# ROXY & JONES

## THE GREAT FAIRYTALE COVER-UP

### ANGELA WOOLFE

WALKER
BOOKS

First published in Great Britain 2020 by Walker Books Ltd
87 Vauxhall Walk, London SE11 5HJ

2 4 6 8 10 9 7 5 3 1

Text © 2020 Angela Woolfe
Cover and interior illustrations © 2020 Paola Escobar

This book has been typeset in Berkeley Oldstyle

Printed and bound by CPI Group (UK) Ltd, Croydon CR0 4YY

British Library Cataloguing in Publication Data:
a catalogue record for this book is available from the British Library

ISBN 978-1-4063-9137-4

www.walker.co.uk

For Lara, who gave me the idea in the first place, with all my love

# WANTED

Pretty, docile girl who needs a place to crash.
Super room available for very little cash!
Applicant must <u>NOT MIND HEIGHTS</u>
   and – vital! – have no issue
With sort of ... disappearing. (Please, <u>NO
   PARENTS</u> who might miss you.)
A fear of witches, truth be told,
   would make arrangements tricky.
But finding any tenant's tough;
   I shouldn't be <u>TOO</u> picky.
Just one more thing: you'll need <u>LONG</u>
   hair – a waterfall of blondeness.
(Oh, dark-haired girls <u>NEED NOT</u> apply.
   For blondes I have more fondness.)
Whoever comes to live here – church-mouse
   poor or filthy rich –
You will really let your hair down! Trust me.

*Trixie T McWitch*

# 1

The Dodgy Old Clock, in the Soup Minister's office above, chimed a quarter to midnight.

Roxy Humperdinck, who was in an underground vault *beneath* the Minister's office, knew that the time was not, in fact, a quarter to midnight.

Her sister, Gretel, who worked as a cleaner at the Ministry, had once told Roxy that the clock on the Minister's desk ran precisely thirteen minutes fast.

So the actual time was eleven thirty-two.

She still had to hurry.

It was dark down here in Storage Vault C, and the torch on Roxy's mobile phone barely dented the gloom. But it had been even darker in the tunnel that led to the vaults, so her eyes were starting to adjust. And at least the clock chime above had given her a rough sense of where she'd ended up. That chilly

9

tunnel deep beneath the Ministry was twisty, dark and *long*. Roxy had lost her bearings several times, and had been relieved to reach the end.

Which was right here, right where she'd hoped to end up: at the storage vaults.

Roxy shone her phone onto the piece of paper she was clutching in her left hand. A sticky label in the top corner declared: **PROPERTY OF STORAGE VAULT C. DO NOT REMOVE**. Beneath this label was the truly weird rhyme she'd read when she'd first spotted the piece of paper, sticking out from under the bath, just a couple of hours ago.

"*Trixie T McWitch…*" she read again now. "It must just be a joke. Witches don't exist. Obviously."

In the gloom of Storage Vault C, at very nearly midnight, it felt a good idea to remind herself of this.

Hold on. Was that … a … rustle?

Probably just a mouse, thought Roxy.

*Please* not a rat.

She wasn't usually the adventuring sort. In fact, she still didn't know quite what had pushed her into coming down here in the first place. It was, frankly, a blur. She'd been brushing her teeth before bed, listening to music through her headphones as she always did, when she'd seen, in the bathroom mirror, that piece of paper sticking out from beneath the bath.

If she'd known when she first pulled it sharply free that doing so was going to result in the bath's side panel coming loose, and that jiggling it to try and fix it was going to result in the panel coming off entirely to reveal a flight of slippery stone steps leading down into somewhere that was quite obviously *not* normal under-bath plumbing ... well, Roxy would probably have ignored the piece of paper and just carried on singing along to the new H-Bomb and the Missiles track blasting into her ears.

But she was here now. Shivering through nerves and from the cold – she was in her pjyamas – and all too aware that she mustn't be long. She had to get safely back to the bathroom before her sister returned from her late-night shift working at the Ministry Ball.

"What am I even *looking for?*" she whispered to herself. More strange rhymes, claiming to be written by witches? It looked like a newspaper advert, but what kind of loon would place a newspaper advert like that? If there were more, would they even be here? Roxy ran the torch all around Vault C. The place could have been picked straight out of a catalogue called Creepy Underground Vaults-R-Us. Seriously. There were dripping stone walls, there was a damp flagstone floor, there were rickety bookshelves crammed with books and files...

11

Maybe the answer lay there. Roxy took a few steps towards one of the shelves.

"Don't move!" commanded a girl's voice from behind it.

Roxy dropped her phone and opened her mouth.

"Well, don't *scream*!" The girl darted round the bookshelf and clapped a small hand over Roxy's mouth. "Do you want every **SMOG** in the Ministry to come running?"

Roxy shook her head for *No*.

"Wait." The girl sounded worried. "Are *you* a **SMOG**?"

Roxy shook her head again for *No*.

"Hmmm." The girl moved her hand away and picked up Roxy's phone. She shone the light in her eyes. "Well, you don't look much like one, I guess. Not unless they've started training fourteen-year-old girls to be elite Soup Ministry Official Guards."

"I'm eleven," Roxy croaked. "Not fourteen."

"*Wow*," said the girl. "You're a funny-looking eleven-year-old."

Which was rude, no matter how you looked at it.

"Here," said the girl, handing the phone back. "I've got a proper torch in my kitbag."

Roxy took her phone and shone the weak light shakily back at her.

The girl was dressed – it was not at all clear *why* – as a giant buttercup.

She was wearing a ruffled blouse in an awful shade of yellow. On her bottom half were violently green knickerbockers, green knee socks and a pair of trainers that looked as if someone had sneezed green snot all over them. Worst of all, though, was her headgear: a bright-yellow bonnet with a huge frill, tied beneath her chin with a shiny yellow ribbon.

"Thing is, you're ever so tall," the girl was saying, as she disappeared, again, round the back of the book-shelf. When she emerged this time, she was carrying a battered leather kitbag that didn't go at all with her awful buttercup costume. "That's why I thought you were older. I'm twelve myself, but I'm titchy, so everyone looks tall to me."

It was true that the girl was incredibly short.

And now that Roxy could see her properly, she realized there was something even more striking about her.

"You're … beautiful!"

"Huh?"

"Your face."

In the flickering phone-light, and once you saw past the blouse and the bonnet, the girl looked like an angel. Her huge eyes were fringed by sweeping lashes, her lips were the shape of a particularly pretty rosebud, her nose was a delicious little button and her skin looked as soft as peach fuzz.

"Oh, *that*." The girl shrugged. "It's actually not as fun as you'd think, looking like this. People get jealous, and stuff. Now *that's* better," she went on, flooding the vault with light as she switched on her torch.

The vault was even bigger than Roxy had thought. The flagstone floor was cracked and had puddles in places, and in one corner there was a flight of wonky stone steps leading up towards a narrow hole in the ceiling.

"Is *that* where you came in?" Roxy asked.

"Yep. Those steps lead up to a false fireplace in the Minister's office."

"But how did you get into the Minister's office in the first place?" Roxy asked. "This whole place is swarming with **SMOGs**. Even more of them than usual tonight, thanks to the Ball the Minister is hosting for Queen Ariadne's birthday."

And the Soup Ministry Official Guards – **SMOGs**, for short – were a pretty terrifying bunch, too. They were armed with Instant Paralysis Lasers, or IPLs, that could turn you to temporary stone with one flash. It had been almost six weeks since Roxy had moved to Rexopolis, and the sight of a **SMOG** patrol still made her anxious.

"Oh, I used a cocktail stick to pick the lock on one of the windows," said the girl, nonchalantly. "I got it from one of the nibbles they were handing round at the Ball. Which. Were. *Awesome*. By the way."

"*You've* been at the Queen's Birthday Ball? In the Ministry ballroom?"

"Yes. Well, not *at* the Ball, as such. More, delivering two hundred silly, frilly cupcakes to the Ball." The girl turned round so that Roxy could see the lettering on the back of her blouse: *Buttercup's Morsels*. "My stepmum's cupcake company. She practically wet herself with excitement when this order came in. Oh, and her name's not Buttercup, by the way, any more than my name's…" She stopped. A suspicious frown creased her face. "Anyway, you seem very interested in this Ball?"

"I'm not really. It's just that it seems like a pretty big deal. My sister is there tonight."

"Oh, lucky *her*. I hope she goes nuts on those nibbles. Because they were excellent. I managed to grab a few from the kitchens when I made my delivery. Sausages-on-sticks … mini sausage rolls … dinky little hot dogs—"

"Nope, she isn't a guest," Roxy interrupted the girl's misty-eyed recollection of sausages past. "She's working at the Ball. She's a cleaner here at the Ministry. Loos, mostly."

"Well, nothing wrong with loo-cleaning. Somebody has to do it, right? And it's probably no less fun than standing around at some boring old party, with the likes of Minister Splendid looking down his massive nose at you. I tell you, you'd never catch *me* partying at a Royal Ball, not even if they served the best nibbles on the *planet*—"

"Sorry," Roxy interrupted again. "I get that you were delivering cupcakes. But I still can't work out what you're doing down *here*. Did you get lost, or something?"

"Course I didn't get lost! And *man*, you do ask a lot of questions! As it happens, *Question Girl*," she went on, looking rather pleased with herself for coming up with this nickname, "I'm grabbing this once-in-a-lifetime opportunity – being here in the Ministry – to find something. Something really important." The girl took a deep breath. "I'm looking for a book."

"You broke into the office of the most important Minister in Illustria for … a *book*?"

The girl nodded.

"You wanted a book about soup *that badly*?"

"I don't want a book about soup at all." The girl sounded bemused. Then she grinned. "Oh, I get it. You *actually think* this is the Ministry for *Soup*."

"But it *is* the Ministry for Soup. What else would it be the Ministry for?"

"Typical." The girl turned back to the shelves, rolling her eyes. "Obviously it's too much to hope that when you bump into a person who's sneaking around a labyrinth of underground tunnels, that person might be *slightly* curious about how this country *really* gets run."

"But I *am* curious!" Roxy exclaimed. "You just called me Question Girl, didn't you?"

"True. How did you get into the tunnels, by the way?"

The girl didn't sound all that interested, but Roxy welcomed the chance to tell *someone* about her extraordinary discovery.

"Well, I was brushing my teeth tonight, in my sister's bathroom ... well, it's *my* bathroom too now, I suppose. I came to live with my sister in the Soup Ministry Staff Quarters a few weeks ago. Anyway, I saw this piece of paper sticking out from under the bath, and when I pulled it, the panel came loose, and then I saw these stairs leading to ... well, I suppose you'd have to call it a *secret tunnel*, really. It must be secret, otherwise my sister would have known about it. And she just thinks the taps don't work, which is why we don't use it, she says. We use someone else's shower three rooms along when we want to wash. Which we do, often, by the way! We're not stinky

17

or anything, just because our bath doesn't work! Anyway, I don't know what I was thinking, really, but when I saw those steps … you kind of *have* to go down a set of mysterious steps into a secret tunnel, right?" Roxy gave an uncertain laugh. "It's the kind of thing that happens in all the books and movies… And to be honest, with my sister working an all-night shift, I guess I thought I should seize the chance. She'd be furious if she knew I'd done this. *Furious*. Plus, well, I've not *done* very much, nothing remotely interesting, really, since I came to Rexopolis. I don't know anyone my own age yet, so…"

"Right." The girl sounded like she was barely listening now, and Roxy could hardly blame her, to be fair, after that long ramble. She looked deep into Roxy's eyes for a moment, without blinking. "Can I trust you?" she asked. Then, before Roxy could reply, she went on, "Actually, I reckon I can. You seem to know nothing about anything, it's quite sweet. And you have a trustworthy sort of face. So are you going to help me look for this book, then?"

Roxy had been about to object to the girl basically calling her ignorant and a bit stupid, but this last question took her by surprise. "Help you? Uh … of course! What's it called?"

The girl drew a ragged breath. Her confidence

seemed to have deserted her for a moment, and she looked, quite suddenly, very small.

"*Mrstabithacattermoleschronicleofthecursedkingdom.*"

Roxy blinked. "Huh?"

"The book. It's called *Mrs Tabitha. Cattermole's. Chronicle. Of. The.*" The girl swallowed hard, as if the words themselves were boulders, and she was struggling under the weight of them. "*Cursed. Kingdom.*"

She pronounced the last-but-one word *curr-said.* Which sounded odd to Roxy.

(Mind you, the whole title sounded odd to Roxy. Plain *weird,* if she was truly honest.)

"A-*ha*!" the girl said suddenly, leaning down to one of the lower shelves. Something had caught her eye, and her bounce seemed to have returned.

Intrigued, Roxy hurried over.

The books on this shelf had leather covers, with peeling gold lettering on the spines, and either the strange girl had suddenly started to give off a faint whiff of mouldering socks, or these books were very old.

"*Voodoo, Hoodoo, Divination and Necromancy* by Nanette Amuse-Bouche ... oh, I read her name somewhere in Dad's notes ... *Magic: A Beginner's Guide* by Phineas Bletherwick ... intriguing, but another time, maybe..."

"They don't sound like books about soup," Roxy began.

"Well, what did I tell you, Question Girl…? *Got* it!"

The girl seized a particularly small leather-bound book and gazed at it.

"Mrs Tabitha," she breathed. "It's you."

It was a tiny bit alarming that the girl was talking to a book.

It was even more alarming that she was calling the book *Mrs Tabitha*.

But Roxy didn't have the time to ponder the weirdness of this. Because just then, in the Minister's office above, the Dodgy Old Clock pinged out the first chimes of midnight.

"*Midnight?*" gasped the girl. "Already?"

"No, no, it's not, actually," began Roxy, "that's just the Dodgy Old …"

"The last bus leaves at quarter past! If I miss it, it's a nine-mile *walk* home. *Man*, I wish I hadn't crashed that delivery bike again!"

"… Clock, and it runs thirteen minutes fast, so it's actually…"

But the girl was already halfway up the stone steps.

"Thanks, Question Girl!" she called over her shoulder before scrabbling through the hole at the top. "Nice knowing you."

And then the fake fireplace slid back into position and the hole closed up behind her.

"Wait!" Roxy called, darting forwards. "You dropped your book!"

Because the girl had accidentally dropped *Mrs Tabitha Cattermole* on the way.

And – in the crazy scramble out of the hole – one of her hideous green trainers had come off.

"Hey!" Roxy called, again. "Can you hear me? Your book's still down here! And you've only got one shoe!"

But it was pointless. The girl had gone. The hole in the ceiling was shut.

Roxy couldn't risk going after her. There would be **SMOG** patrols up there, trigger-happy with their IPLs. Besides, she just wanted to get safely back to bed. The vault seemed blacker than ever now that the bright torchlight was gone, and she felt foolish and silly in her dressing-gown and slippers, on her half-baked attempt at adventure.

Mind you, maybe it wasn't *that* half-baked. She had discovered this *Mrs Tabitha Cattermole* book, after all.

The strange girl had risked the **SMOG** patrols to come and find it. There must be *something* exciting in it. Something adventure-worthy. Something way more interesting (and hopefully a lot less creepy) than fake witches advertising for a roommate.

Roxy put the old book into her dressing-gown pocket and – because she didn't know what else to do with it – shoved the vile green trainer into the gap on the shelf where the book had been.

Then, holding her phone up in front of her as if it might protect her from the dark rather than merely pierce it, Roxy hurried out of Storage Vault C and back into the inky tunnel.

## 2

### FOODSTUFFS IN THE CURSED KINGDOM, FROM THE TYME OF THE HUNDRED YEARS' SLUMBER TO THE DARK DAYES OF THE PERPETUAL WICKEDNESS

The humble parsnip, truth to tell, was served at ev'ry meal;

    'Twas mostly boiled (or, sometimes, mashed, if boiled did not appeal).

    This unpretentious tuber graced the Kingdom's finest tables (except the Gilded Palace, where 'twas only served in stables).

23

And by and by, there came a fad for spreading it
on toast.

For simple, hearty food was what the people
loved the most.

The meadowes of the south were where the
largest parsnips grew.

Those cultivated here were thought the finest
kind for stew.

Whilst on the Blizzy Lizzies, where the air was
cold and dry,

The parsnips pluck'd from out the soil were
mostly served in pie.

The parsnips of the east were rather soft, and
bland, and stodgy.

Consumed in hefty quantities, they'd make one's
tummy dodgy.

But glad to say, the parsnips that were grown in

Roxy stopped reading. It had taken her the past five
days to struggle through the entire book once. Now
she was struggling through the whole thing all over
again, just to be absolutely certain that she hadn't accidentally missed something – *anything* – interesting the
first time around.

There had been seventy-three chapters just as dull as this one.

There were thirty-six chapters even duller to come.

The *entire book*, apart from one random page (maybe Mrs Tabitha had been having a rare Normal Person Day) was written in verse.

Yep. *Verse*. That rhymed. Just like Trixie T McWitch's weird roommate advert that was still crumpled up in Roxy's dressing-gown pocket.

But this interesting coincidence didn't actually make the book one iota more interesting. It was in fact so STOMACH-ACHINGLY TEDIOUS that it almost made Roxy want to actually read the week-old copy of *Royal Rumorz* magazine that she was only using to disguise *Mrs Tabitha Cattermole*.

*Almost.*

"He is *so lush*," came a breathy voice from across the room.

It belonged to Bijou Splendid, whose bedroom Roxy was in.

Bijou was perched at her pink dressing table skimming a *Royal Rumorz* of her own.

*Her* copy of the magazine was the very newest, hot-off-the-press edition. Bijou was always hot off the press. She had her own MeMeMeTeeVee channel, where she presented a super-popular vlog called *B's*

*Buzz*. Here she discussed the latest celebrity gossip, doled out fashion tips and said mean things about people she didn't like.

Bijou could get away with saying mean things – indeed, Bijou only had a super-popular vlog in the first place – because her father was Atticus Splendid, Soup Minister.

"Roxy?" Bijou snapped now, when Roxy didn't respond. "Are you still there?"

"Yep, Bijou. Still here," said Roxy from the squishy depths of a pink glittery beanbag.

Roxy wasn't a fan of pink. Or glitter. Or Bijou, come to think of it. But when Bijou had first noticed her yesterday morning, sitting with her book and her headphones in a quiet part of the Ministry's famous courtyard garden, Roxy hadn't felt able to turn down the invitation to hang out.

Partly because it hadn't been an invitation so much as a command.

But also because, when all was said and done, Roxy was new in Rexopolis. And she was freakishly tall for her age. With weird springy hair that stood up in loo-brush tufts, no matter how much she tried to coax it not to. And in a month's time, when the holidays ended and she finally took up the place her sister Gretel had found for her at the nearest school,

Roxy would be heading to class every day with Bijou Splendid. So while she might not want Bijou as a friend, she certainly didn't want her as an enemy.

"Then tell me what you think of this Spencer Sparke-Plugg poster." Bijou was brandishing her magazine.

Roxy forced herself to look interested as she peered across the room at Bijou's magazine page.

The photo of Spencer Sparke-Plugg looked pretty much like all the other posters of the cheesy pop star that adorned the pink bedroom: way too much tan and way, way too many teeth.

"Oh, it's great." Roxy stuck up a vague thumb, hoping that now she'd be left in peace so she could concentrate on *Mrs Tabitha*.

Not that there was much peace, thanks to the music blaring out from Bijou's speakers. Even more sadly, this music was – of course – Spencer Sparke-Plugg.

Bijou began to croon to the pop star's latest track as she tore out the poster and tacked it to her mirror. *"She got that pale green skin (and she knows it!)... She givin' me those evils... I'll never get ooooouuuuuuut-a-heeeere..."*

"You know that's a cover version, right?" Roxy couldn't help saying, although she regretted it as soon as the words were out of her mouth. "I mean, it's originally an H-Bomb and the Missiles song. A classic, in fact."

"Whatevs." Bijou rolled her eyes. "Spencer's version is *way* better than all the wailing in the original. You can *dance* to it!"

"Yes. Um, I'm not sure it's *meant* to be danced to. If you listen to the lyrics, they're actually quite—"

"Are you a Spencer Sparke-Plugg fan or not?" Bijou snapped, putting down her magazine and glaring at Roxy in the mirror.

"Huh? Oh. Yeah. Huge fan. Huge." This was a huge *fib*. Roxy hoped it wasn't obvious. She'd gone too far out on a limb with the whole H-Bomb comment; she could see that now. What was *wrong* with her? She wanted to fit in, so why hadn't she just kept her mouth shut?

"And who else do you like?" Bijou stabbed a finger at another of the tanned, toothy boys in her poster collection. "Do you like him?"

"Oh, yes, love him." Roxy didn't have the faintest clue who "him" was, so she winged it. "Adore his music. That latest track … I mean, wow."

Bijou swivelled on her dressing-table stool and stared at Roxy as if she'd just vomited all over the pink glittery beanbag. (Which might have improved it.)

"*That's* not a musician. That's the *prince*. Queen Ariadne's *son*."

"Right. I know that. I … thought you were pointing at someone else…"

"You don't seem to know much *important stuff*," said Bijou, her small eyes narrowing. "Where did you say you're from, again?"

"Um, well, my dad moves around a lot. The last place we lived was Daisyfield, near the border with Shiny-Newland. Before that we lived in Mount Pleasant for a couple of years, and before *that* we lived abroad, in Parvenia, actually, and before that…" Roxy was blabbing. She was a nervous blabber. "I moved here to Rexopolis – to the Ministry, obviously – a few weeks ago. To live with my sister."

"Well, where do you live in the Ministry?" Bijou snapped. "Not those grotty horrible staff quarters, with all the cleaners and stuff?"

"Yeah, in the grotty horrible staff quarters," Roxy admitted, feeling a stab of guilt. It wasn't Gretel's fault she was a loo-cleaner, after all, and if it weren't for her sister inviting her to live in those very same *grotty horrible staff quarters* … well, she didn't know where she'd be right now. Her brand-new stepmother had made it clear there was to be no bedroom for Roxy in the flashy new house her dad was building for her in Bronze Beach, on the north-western coast of Illustria. (And her father, as usual, had simply gone along with whatever his latest wife wanted.)

"My sister's a cleaner here," she added, lifting her

chin. "And actually, the staff quarters aren't that bad. We won't even be there for much longer. We'll need a bigger place, now that I'm here for good—"

Bijou held up a hand, halting Roxy's fresh attack of blab-mouth.

"Daddy would freak," she said, "if he knew I had the *cleaner's* sister in my bedroom."

Roxy could – should, in fact – have taken offence at this and marched out of the room.

But something else Bijou had said stopped her.

*Daddy* was, of course, Atticus Splendid, Soup Minister.

If there had been one thing Roxy hadn't been able to shake off since that night in the vault – apart from the musty smell of damp socks, of course – it had been something the cupcake-delivery girl had said about the Ministry above them.

*You actually think this is the Ministry for Soup.*

Maybe Roxy – who had recently, after all, been given the nickname Question Girl – could learn something interesting from hanging out with Bijou after all.

"Uh, Bijou –" she tried to sound casual – "you know how obviously you're *the* person who knows everything going on around here …"

"So, like, I'm not saying you can *never* hang out with me or anything …" Bijou was pouting at herself in the

30

pink mirror now, twisting her hair into a high ponytail.

Roxy continued "… haven't *you* ever wondered – or asked your dad, maybe – why there actually *is* a Soup Minister at all…?"

"… but it would probably be better if you just, like, didn't do it very *often* …"

"… because …" *Deep breath, Roxy.* "I don't know if you've ever actually noticed, but there doesn't seem to *be* very much soup around Rexopolis. Around the whole of Illustria, in fact. I've lived in this country pretty much my entire life, and I've only eaten soup maybe twice in that entire time. And it was plain old cream-of-tomato. Not exactly unusual. And now that I'm actually living here in the Ministry, it's occurred to me that it's a bit weird to have an *entire Ministry* in charge of any kind of soup at all."

"… and anyway, I've got to film my next vlog post for *B's Buzz* in a few minutes, so you'd better go." Bijou sauntered over to the beanbag. "I'll need this," she added, reaching down and grabbing the copy of *Royal Rumorz* from Roxy's hand. "There's a 'Which Hottie Is the One for You?' quiz in there. I want to do it live."

There was a thud, and then a strong smell of damp socks.

*Mrs Tabitha Cattermole* had slipped out of the magazine and fallen to the floor.

Bijou stared. "What's *that*?"

"Oh, nothing! Just a book!" Roxy grabbed for it, but not fast enough. Bijou had grabbed it herself and was holding it at arm's length.

"It smells of … *Ewwww…!* What *is* that?"

"Damp socks," Roxy jabbered, seeing an opportunity. "Really stinky, vile socks that have been mouldering away on someone's cheesy feet for ages. So if you just give it back to me, pretty much right now-ish, I'll take it far, far…"

Bijou's eyes were practically popping out of her head. "Is it –" her voice became a whisper – "*old*?"

"Old?" Roxy echoed. "Yeah, it's old. But it's *really* bor—"

"*SECURITEEEEEEEEEEEEEEEEEEEE!*" screeched Bijou.

And then the bedroom door burst open, and four ginormous **SMOGs** barrelled through.

**3**

"Do you have *any idea*," Gretel asked Roxy, "what you've *done*?"

It was the very early hours of the next morning and the sisters were home, in Gretel's tiny bedsit in the Soup Ministry staff quarters.

Despite the fact that it was smaller and drabber than anywhere Roxy had ever lived, she had still been relieved to return here a few minutes ago. After the hours she'd just spent in the Ministry's Decontamination Zone, this place felt *fabulous*.

"Do you have any idea," Gretel went on, "of the trouble you've caused? The strings I had to pull to get you out of that place?"

"Strings?"

"Favours I've had to promise." Gretel wasn't looking at her; she was too busy removing her cleaning overalls and stripy scarf, and pulling on her fluffy bunny slippers. "I'll be paying the price for your little escapade from now until Christmas!"

"Sorry," Roxy said, for (what felt like, but probably wasn't quite) the fifty millionth time. "I truly am, Gretel. But what do you mean, you've had to promise favours?"

"I don't *know yet*, Roxy! Someone will probably make me work all the really unpopular shifts or something. You don't need to know any more about it. Did they feed you?"

"Huh?"

"In the DZ – I mean, the Decontamination Zone. Did they give you anything to eat?"

"No. There wasn't time. As soon as we got there, they started hosing us down with these big jets of water, and then they took away my clothes and gave me this –" Roxy pulled at the papery yellow jumpsuit she'd been told to wear – "and then they put me in this kind of creepy white *cell* for about three hours, and…"

"OK, I get it. You haven't eaten." Gretel reached into a cupboard on the wall that was only just visible among all Roxy's music posters. It was where she kept her allergy medicine, her knitting and a few of her dreary snacks. "Here. Eat."

Silently, Roxy took the packet of Proon Puffs that

Gretel was holding out for her and sat down on the end of Gretel's bed. She was hungrier than she'd ever been in her life. Hungrier, even, than that time when Dad and Lindsey (Stepmother Number ... was it Six?) had gone away for the week, locking the front door behind them and forgetting to leave Roxy with a key. So she didn't even care that Proon Puffs were the least delicious breakfast cereal on the planet. At least they were *food*.

"I mean, what were you thinking, Roxy? Breaking into an underground vault!"

"I didn't *break in*. I followed a tunnel. From *your* bathroom, incidentally. And by the way, G, did you already know why that bath doesn't work? Did you know about the loose panel and the steps?"

"Of course I didn't, Roxy! I spend all day cleaning bathrooms. The last thing I ever think about is my own!" Gretel glanced towards the door that led to the bathroom, looking as if she'd happily board the whole room up right now if she had some wood and a hammer handy. "I had absolutely no idea anything like *that* was down there. It's some supply tunnels from the olden days, I gather. It'll be sealed off, by the way, as soon as one of the Ministry handymen has the time."

"I was just intrigued, that's all." Roxy stared at the

floor. (Actually, she stared at her thin mattress, which almost entirely covered the floor.) "It's not like there's anything exciting for me to do around here."

"Hey, it's not my fault I have to work such long hours, you know. I have two of us to think about these days!" Gretel, looking more-than-usually weary and cross, perched on the other end of the mattress. "So what exactly did the Minister say when he came to talk to you?"

This had been, among many hairy-scary moments, the hairiest and scariest of them all: Minister Atticus Splendid himself, appearing in Roxy's cell.

"Well, it was weird." Roxy's stomach rumbled, and she remembered she was supposed to be eating the Proon Puffs. She took a big handful. "He mostly just told me off for upsetting Bijou."

"So he didn't mention … *old* stuff?"

"Actually, he did. And that's exactly what *he* called it too!"

*I hope you're not going to waste any more of your time looking for old stuff,* the Soup Minister had said, beetling at her out of his pale, watery eyes. He had looked very, very large in the small cell and very, VERY orange against the bright-white tiles and floor. *And I do hope you aren't going to tell anyone else about it. Nobody's interested, for one thing.*

"Well, nobody's really interested in old stuff," said Gretel.

"Mmm," said Roxy. She chewed for a moment longer, then, as Gretel stood up to get her pyjamas, she went on, "The thing is, though, Gretel; if nobody's interested, why was I rushed off to be *decontaminated* in the first place?"

"Because of that stinky old book you took – *stole*, I don't need to remind you – from the vault! Heaven only knows what terrible mould spores were all over that thing!"

"*That's* what the Ministry needs an entire Decotamination *Zone* for? In case some old book gets taken off a shelf?"

"No, I'm sure it's—"

"You've always told me Illustria is the cleanest, tidiest, safest place to live in the entire world! Why does it need a Decontamination Zone? In the *Soup* Ministry, of all places. And another thing –" Roxy was exhausted, but her brain was buzzing – "why did Minister Splendid himself come and quiz me about it all? I mean, I don't know how much you see of the Soup Minister when you're cleaning his loo (not much, if you're lucky) but does he strike you as the kind of man who usually bothers chatting with eleven-year-olds?"

"Roxy—"

"And you should have seen how relieved he looked when I agreed that old stuff was really boring, and that I'd never talk about it again. *And* how happy he looked when I told him I'd not really understood anything I read in *Mrs Tabitha Cattermole* anyway."

"Roxy—"

"And then as he was leaving, just before he shut the door behind him, I heard him telling someone they could *cancel Mrs Smith now* … whoever *that* might be … and then he said, *Obviously we've got WAY bigger fish to fry right now* – which, OK, is probably the *most* soup-related thing I heard him say, if he was talking about actual fish, which I'm pretty sure he wasn't, and then—"

"Roxy!" Gretel bellowed. "That's enough!"

Which was a shock, because Gretel never bellowed. She was one of the quietest and most mouse-like people Roxy had ever known. Actually, with her pebbly glasses and her blinking, she was actually more *mole*-like than mouse-like.

"For the last time," she went on, "there is ABSOLUTELY NOTHING SUSPICIOUS GOING ON IN THE MINISTRY FOR SOUP! There are *no conspiracies*. There is *no dark and thrilling intrigue*. There is *nobody called Mrs Smith*. There is only soup. Do you understand, Roxy?"

"But, Gretel—"

"ONLY SOUP!" roared her sister.

There was a short, uncomfortable silence, during which Gretel put a Proon Puff into her mouth and crunched it irritably.

"Ugh!" She spat it into her hand. "Have they changed the recipe? This tastes awful!"

"No, but … OK, I sprinkled in a bit of sugar when I first opened the pack the other day…"

"SUGAR?" As always, the mere mention of the sweet stuff looked as if it might make Gretel faint. "*How* many times have I told you, Roxy?"

"That sugary cereal is dangerous? That sugary *anything* is dangerous? Roughly, ten bazillion times." Roxy banged the packet down so hard that several bone-dry Puffs actually flew into the air. "I mean, in the name of Diabolica, Gretel, can you PLEASE just CHILL OUT about everything?"

Gretel's eyes flew wide.

"Where in the world," she asked, in a low, warning voice that sounded nothing like her usual apologetic mumble, "did you hear the expression *in the name of Diabolica*?"

"What? Oh… It was in *Mrs Tabitha Cattermole*. That musty old book that's caused all this fuss."

To be precise, it had been written on page

one hundred and sixty-two, halfway through CHAPTER THE NYNETEENTH: EPITHETS, SLANDERS AND OBLOQUYS FROM ONE TUESDAY MORNING IN 1489 TO 8.33 a.m. (OR THEREABOUTS) ON THE 9th OF AUGUST, 1743:

And in the towns and villages, when something bad occurred, "In the name of Diabolica!" was very often heard...

"For. The. Very. Last. Time –" Gretel, now a lot less "mole" and a lot more "fire-breathing dragon", banged out every word on the door with the flat of her hand – "It. Is. Not. A. Ridiculous. Fuss. It. Is. Not. Even. A. Sensible. Fuss. It. Is. As. Far. From. Any. Kind. Of. Fuss. As. It. Is. Possible. To. Be. And. If. You. Keep. Asking. These. Kinds. Of. Questions. I. Will. Lose. My. Job. And. We. Will. Have. Nowhere. To. Live. So. You. Will. Have. To. Go. Back. And. Live. With. Dad. And. His. New. Wife. Even. Though—"

Gretel stopped herself, just in time.

"Even though Dad and Mindy don't want me," said Roxy, but so quietly that she couldn't be sure Gretel had even heard.

There was another short silence.

"I just need to know," said Gretel, tightly, "that you've understood what I'm saying."

"OK, OK!" said Roxy. The whole Diabolica thing

40

had really freaked her sister out. "I get it. I'll stop asking questions!" She reached for her phone and headphones, crammed onto Gretel's tiny bedside table, and pulled the headphones on.

Just as swiftly, Gretel pulled them back off.

"You can't just hide behind your music, Roxy. You have to actually listen to me on this."

"I'm listening!" Roxy held up her hands.

"And you won't go sneaking into underground tunnels beneath the Ministry ever again?"

"I won't go sneaking into underground tunnels beneath the Ministry ever again."

"Because there's nothing to look for…"

There was a sudden sharp bleep from Gretel's overalls. She grabbed her phone from the pocket.

What she saw on the screen made her face turn from its usual pallid grey to white.

"I have to go," she mumbled. "Work. An emergency."

"A *cleaning* emergency?" Roxy stared at her. "At one thirty in the morning? Two nights in a row?"

Gretel's working hours were weird, yes, and superlong, double yes, but this was ridiculous. Roxy had been woken by the ping of Gretel's phone *last* night, too, at which Gretel had sprung out of bed like a sunburnt penguin, disappeared into the darkness and not come home until almost sunrise.

"Yeah. There's been a really, really bad spillage. Stuff everywhere."

Seeing as Gretel's cleaning responsibilities were mostly toilets, Roxy decided that she *really* didn't want to hear any more about this.

"I have to go." Deep lines were etched in Gretel's forehead. "I could be a while."

Roxy said nothing. She simply watched as Gretel flung off her bunny slippers and yanked on her ugly rubber work-clogs, then pulled on her overalls and wrapped her striped scarf several times round her neck.

"You go to sleep, Roxy. I'll see you in the morning. Oh –" Gretel paused by the door. "NO LEAVING THE MINISTRY, ROXY. No exploring. And *absolutely no tunnels.*"

"OK, OK!" said Roxy, putting her headphones back on and scrolling through her phone to her playlists. "Deal."

Gretel let out the longest and dreariest sigh of all the long and dreary sighs Roxy had ever heard her utter. Then she pushed her pebbly glasses up to the bridge of her nose and closed the door behind her.

**4**

When Roxy awoke, to a ping from her phone, there was a Proon Puff up her nose.

Her head felt soggy, as if someone had snuck in during the night and filled it with quicksand, and it took several sleepy minutes to work the stray Puff out of her left nostril. She had only just succeeded when she noticed the note stuck to the door: *Came back at 8 a.m. but you were still asleep,* it said, in Gretel's neat handwriting. *Heading off for usual shift now. Get your lunch in staff canteen – fish pie today! And if you insist on having pudding, please avoid the custard – the stuff's absolutely loaded with sugar!!!*

Here Gretel had drawn an awkward smiley face that was – Roxy knew – her way of saying sorry that Roxy would be on her own all day.

*And remember what I said last night,* the note went

43

on, the pencil line thickening for emphasis. *No going into that tunnel. And do not leave the ministry grounds, Roxy, or there will be big trouble.*

There was a short PS: *But get a bit of fresh air, will you? Please don't just sit around in your pyjamas listening to loud music all day.*

Roxy stared at it, wishing she could shake off the quicksand feeling in her head.

"Fresh air," she muttered, pulling on random clothes and then reaching for her phone and her headphones. "She's right. That's what I need. Fresh air. *And* loud music."

A quick glance at the phone showed her that the pinging had been Dad. He'd sent one of his guilty flurries of messages:

**8.18 a.m.** – Hey, kiddo! We're back from honeymoon! Promise we'll get that guest room ready soon, and you can spend the weekend! Dad xx

**8.22 a.m.** – Mindy says it definitely won't be before Christmas, though. Dad xx

**8.23 a.m.** – Actually, Mindy's just told me there's a good chance it won't be before Easter. Dad xx

**8.27 a.m.** – Oh, btw, check out our new family SelfSpace page, tons of good honeymoon pics on there! I'll send the log-in. Dad xx

**8.42 a.m.** – Actually, Mindy would prefer you didn't have the log-in. Privacy and stuff, you know? Dad xx

**8.56 a.m.** – Actually, Mindy thinks it might be more useful if we turned the guest room into a nice home gym. Or just somewhere she can paint her toenails. Still, there's always a comfy sofa for you to crash on, if you ever fancy a quick visit! Dad xx

**9.04 a.m.** – Actually, Mindy says she has strict rules about people sleeping on the sofa. Dad xx

**9.54 a.m.** – See you around, kiddo. Dad xx

Roxy deleted them all. It would be the last she heard from him for weeks. More, probably, if he and her new stepmother set off on another luxury cruise.

Mindy was Stepmother Number – Roxy often lost count – Eleven? And she was even more fond of spending Dad's considerable fortune than her predecessors.

As she went outside, Roxy shoved on her headphones and turned up the volume on her phone.

Some Parvenian hip-hop, she decided, from the brand-new playlist her brother had sent her. Music would clear the fog in her head. It always did.

And lo and behold, as soon as the super-loud hip-hop blasted into her ears, last night's unanswered question popped back, clear as crystal: *Why oh why oh why had a boring old snore-fest of a book like* Mrs Tabitha Cattermole *caused such panic at the Ministry?*

(Not that it would ever cause a panic anywhere ever again. The book had been taken away. Roxy had overheard a high-ranking **SMOG** ordering it to be *destroyed. Burnt, in fact. The Minister thought it had been done years ago, so this time he actually wants to see the pile of ash. All right?*)

"I don't care what Gretel says," she muttered. "Something *is* going on around here. Weird stuff. Freaky stuff. *Secret* stuff the Ministry for Soup is trying to hide."

"… if you'd all like to follow me this way," came a voice, loud enough to slice through the hip-hop. "We are now entering the exquisite courtyard garden of the Soup Ministry."

It was the 10 a.m. Royal Rexopolis Guided Tour.

Since Roxy had moved in with Gretel, she had seen a great number of these hourly tours trooping their way around this part of town. They began at Mrs Kettleman's Traditional Custarde Doughnut Emporium on Mulligatawny Square, crossed the Square to visit the Soup Ministry gardens, then headed back out again to see the artworks in the King's Gallery, before finishing with selfies on the steps of the gilded Royal Palace at the other end of the Square.

46

This morning's tour was a school group: fifty bored-looking kids meandering through the Ministry courtyard, taking photos with their phones and dripping Traditional Custarde all down their "I ♥ Rexopolis" T-shirts.

Roxy pulled up her hoodie – school groups always made her self-conscious – and made her way to her favourite spot: the stone step at the bottom of the gold-plated statue of Atticus Splendid. Here it was always dry and protected a little from the breeze, thanks to the size of the statue above.

"Yeah, so that's a statue of Minister Splendid," the tour guide was saying through a wireless microphone. "Best Soup Minister Illustria has ever had, if you're one of those weird people who actually think soup is important. In fact, I'm pretty sure he's the *only* Soup Minister Illustria has ever had. So every time you tuck into a hearty bowl of chicken-noodle broth, you can thank your lucky stars that Minister Splendid has worked tirelessly to pass some law to ensure there's enough of the chicken and not too much of the noodle."

Roxy glanced up, startled. The tour guides usually adopted a particularly reverential tone for the statue. She'd certainly never heard any of them talk *this* way about the Minister.

"Um, excuse me?" one of the girls in the group was asking as they all filed past, clicking their camera-phones in the vague direction of the statue. "Is Minister Splendid's daughter the one that does B's Buzz? Because I *love* her vlog on MeMeMeTeeVee, she's so stylish and—"

"Abigail!" This was from the teacher at the back. "We're here to find out about *history*. And *culture*. Not silly celebrity nonsense."

"Yeah," said the tour guide. This came out more like a "Ymmuumph..." (Roxy couldn't actually see the guide at the front of the group as she was so short, but it sounded like she was midway through a Traditional Custarde Doughnut herself.) "History and culture. Which is why I'm thinking: we should've got more doughnuts."

As the group shifted, Roxy finally caught a glimpse of the tour guide. She was smaller than most of the schoolchildren, and she was muffled up against the brisk weather in a huge scarf that hid most of the lower part of her face. The rest of it was hidden by a tour guide's baseball cap, which was pulled down almost to the tip of her nose.

"Excuse me!" The teacher sounded appalled. "This tour is supposed to be educational! Didn't you *just agree* that the children are here to learn the history and culture of our great capital?"

"But Mrs Kettleman has been selling those custard doughnuts for *years*," said the tour guide. "That's historical as far as I'm concerned."

Roxy laughed. She couldn't help it.

At the sound of the laugh, which rang out rather loudly in the square, the tour guide's baseball cap swivelled towards Roxy.

She was staring.

Staring HARD.

"You know what," the teacher said, glowering down at the tiny guide, "I think I'll just give your office a call and see if they'll send out a different tour guide. You seem awfully *young*, to be frank, and—"

"No!" The tour guide's attention moved swiftly back to her group. "Don't do that! Don't call them! You want history? You want culture? Then go take a good old look at … uh, I dunno … that tree."

"What tree?" asked the teacher.

"That one right over there." The guide waved her microphone. "Big, oaky-looking thing, near those *Keep off the Grass* signs. Fascinating tree, that. Very historical. And cultural! And … that vlog person, B, or C, or whatever her name is, she hangs out beneath that tree all the time. I think she might even have carved her name into it."

"OK, this is getting ridiculous," began the teacher. "Children, *do not go over to that tree*. We need to return to the bus. *Children!*"

But the schoolchildren, phones at the ready, were already stampeding across the cobblestones towards the random tree on the far side of the courtyard.

As the teacher jogged after them, the tour guide made for the statue.

Roxy got to her feet.

"Sorry, I'm probably not even supposed to sit here. I'll find somewhere else..."

But the tour guide wasn't listening. She was pulling off her baseball cap and scarf to reveal the face beneath.

She wasn't a tour guide at all. She was just a girl.

And not just any old girl.

She was the cupcake-delivery girl Roxy had met five days ago in the vault.

**5**

"Oh, wow … it's you! The girl in the buttercup costume."

"No. Well, yeah. But not any more, thank goodness." The girl pulled off the microphone. "Call me Jones."

"*Jones?*"

"Yep." The girl – Jones – regarded Roxy coolly, with bright cornflower eyes. She had dyed her blonde hair – it wasn't clear why – a shade that was not quite black but more of a midnight blue. "So. It's you. Question Girl. From the vault."

"Yes. I'm Roxy. Roxy Humperdinck. Sorry, I'm confused. Are you … a *tour guide* now?"

Jones let out a *ppffft* noise. "Course not. I borrowed this uniform. Wait a minute. Does it count as borrowing if I didn't ask the owner first?"

51

"Um, that sounds a tiny bit more like stealing?"

"Right. Did you know you've got something on your face?"

"My face?" Roxy put up a hand, self-consciously, and felt two dry lumps beneath her left eye – it was a couple more Proon Puffs. The box must have spilled over in her bed after she'd dropped off: the blasted Puffs had ended up everywhere. "Proon Puffs," she said, feeling her face redden. "Breakfast cereal."

"I'm starving! Can I try one?"

Jones took a Puff from Roxy, popped it in her mouth and spat it straight out.

"It's like rock! What do they make them from?"

"Yeah, they are a bit dry," agreed Roxy.

Though, as she peered more closely at the grey-ish object Jones was handing back to her, she realized that this one wasn't, in fact, a Proon Puff at all. It might indeed have been made of rock – though a tough ceramic was more likely – and it looked more like the dreary, educational free giveaways that came in the Puffs packet. The last box had contained a plain, practical eraser; in the last-but-one box there'd been a plain, practical pencil. This time around, the gift appeared to be mathematics-themed: an isosceles triangle that you were probably meant to use your plain, practical pencil to draw around, or something. Roxy didn't know, and couldn't care less. She shoved the little rocky shape into her pocket.

"I don't think that was actually a Proon Puff," she mumbled, embarrassed.

"Either way," said Jones, "I'll stick with Honey Nugz, if it's all the same to you."

"It's … it's good to see you again," Roxy blurted out. "I didn't think I would."

"Likewise. And I didn't plan to come back to the Ministry, trust me. I'm only here today because…" Jones lowered her voice. "OK, we have to be careful. But you remember *that book* I was looking for, the night we met?"

Roxy's stomach plummeted. "You know, it's funny you should mention that book, because—"

"Well, I somehow managed to drop the blooming thing somewhere, didn't I? And one of my trainers – though, to be honest, I didn't notice *that* until I got home. Happens quite a lot. I've got one foot smaller than the other. Anyway, the reason I'm back, brilliantly disguised as an official Ministry guide –" Jones was whispering so softly now that she was really just mouthing the words – "is so I can try to get past the **SMOGs**, sneak down to Vault C again and get that book back."

Roxy's stomach plummeted a little further.

She laughed from nerves.

"The thing is, Jones, that … well, the book isn't there."

"What?"

"*Mrs Tabitha Cattermole*. It's not in the vault any more."

"Then where is it?"

"Well, I kind of have it…"

Jones opened her eyes extremely wide.

"You're joking me," she said.

"I'm not."

"Then can *I* have it?"

"No. I mean, not exactly."

"What in the name of Diabolica," Jones said, "are you blithering about?"

"Hey!" Roxy was diverted. "What was that? About Diabolica?"

"It's just an expression," Jones grunted. "Forget it."

"But I'd never heard it before, and now that's twice in one week! From you, and in *Mrs Tabitha Cattermole*."

"You've read *Mrs Tabitha Cattermole*?"

"Yes. Which is why I'm trying to tell you, it doesn't matter that it's been destroyed, burned actually, because I have it all…"

Roxy stopped. But not soon enough.

This was not how she had planned to tell Jones the

tragic fate of her precious book.

Jones's face was now a shade of grey similar to the miserable educational isosceles triangle from the box of Proon Puffs.

"What," she croaked, "did you just say?"

"It's kind of a funny story…"

"*MRS TABITHA CATTERMOLE'S CHRONICLE OF THE CURSED KINGDOM* has been BURNED?" Jones yelled.

Then she seemed to remember that they were standing right out in the open, in the heart of the Ministry.

She grabbed Roxy by the elbow and, with surprising strength for someone so tiny, dragged her round to the other side of Atticus Splendid's statue. This put them way, way closer to the Minister's gold-plated bottom than Roxy cared to be, but she wasn't about to say so.

"*How in the name of Diabolica did that happen?*" Jones hissed. Her cornflower-blue eyes were wild. She looked somewhere between incandescently angry and tremendously distressed.

"OK, it got kind of … confiscated. And then Minister Splendid came along – to this special Decontamination Zone I'd been dragged off to, when they found I had the book – and he told them to destroy it. Apparently he thought it had been destroyed years ago. But if you just *listen to me* for a minute," Roxy gabbled, "you'll realize that it doesn't matter if the *actual* book has been destroyed. Because I still *have* the book!"

She tapped her forehead with the tip of an index finger.

Jones stared at her.

There was a moment of awed silence.

Then Jones grabbed Roxy by the hoodie.

"I am going," she announced, through gritted teeth, "to actually kill you."

Ah. So it hadn't been an awed silence after all.

"It's true!" gasped Roxy. "I have the entire book in my head, I swear! It's this freaky thing I do! I remember stuff! Every word I've ever read, in fact!"

Jones let go of Roxy's collar and returned her, with a bump, to the marble cobbles.

"Load of pig poo," she said.

But her eyes were fixed on Roxy's face.

"It isn't pig poo," said Roxy. "I have this … well, I don't know how to describe it. A gift, I suppose. I only need to look at a page for a few seconds and I remember what's written on it for the rest of my life."

"Whoa, whoa, whoa." Jones held up a hand. "Are you serious? You can remember *every word you've ever read*?"

56

Roxy nodded.

"But … *how?*"

"I don't know," Roxy said. "I just do. I can't help it. I can't *stop* it. And I usually keep quiet about it, by the way. I worry people will think I'm weird."

Jones chewed her lower lip for a moment. Then she turned, sharply, and began to walk away.

This had creeped Jones out so much that she was just *leaving?*

This was bad. Yes, Jones was a tiny bit terrifying. And sarcastic. And weirdly obsessed with doughnuts. And sausages. And breakfast cereal.

But she was also fascinating, and mysterious, and … well, a whole lot more fun to talk to than the likes of Bijou Splendid.

"You coming?" Jones paused, on her way towards the archway that led out of the Ministry courtyard.

"Huh?" said Roxy.

"Are you coming with me?" Jones said. "Back to my place. Which happens to be right above Mrs Kettleman's. Where they're taking today's Special out of the oven right about now. Twice-Glazed Caramel. Just in case you were wondering."

There were many things Roxy was trying to get her mouth to say. Things like: *I've just told you your precious book's been destroyed and that I have a freaky talent for remembering every single word I've ever read, and you're talking about Twice-Glazed Caramel Custarde Doughnuts?*

But instead she found herself uttering just one word.

"Yes."

**6**

Jones's "place" was an attic directly above Mrs Kettleman's Traditional Custarde Doughnut Emporium. This was probably why it smelled strongly of Custarde Doughnuts.

Though this could also have been something to do with all the empty doughnut boxes littered about the room, or the occasional half-chewed doughnut or heap of crumbs.

Roxy hovered uncertainly at the door as Jones strode inside.

"I'll just grab one thing," said Jones, crossing the rickety wood-plank floor to a small suitcase in the corner. "Then we'll head downstairs and order up a plate of those Twice-Glazed Caramel bad boys while we talk."

Which gave Roxy a chance, while Jones flung

things out of the case, to gaze around.

The attic was a mess.

It wasn't just the doughnut paraphernalia. Almost every brick of the wall was covered with sheets of writing-paper, on which were scribbled notes and drawings. One *entire* wall was covered with a huge yellowing map: its curling corners depicted a country the exact size and shape of Illustria, but it was apparently *not* Illustria, because **MAP OF THE CK** was clearly written at the top. There was no furniture, not even a bed – in fact, it looked like, if Jones slept at all, she slept in that pile of thin blankets beside that tiny electric heater. The rest of the floor was taken up with gigantic pieces of torn-up cardboard box. On these were even more scribbles: flow charts, pie charts, incomprehensible graphs and, in one case, just the words written, in red marker: **IF YOU ONLY REMEMBER ONE THING, MAKE IT THIS: TRUST NO ONE!!!!!!!!!!**

Which made it quite nice, Roxy couldn't help thinking, that Jones apparently trusted *her*.

"Great place," she said politely (because she felt she had to say *something*. She got the impression Jones wasn't exactly used to having visitors).

"What? Oh, yeah, it's awesome." For once, Jones didn't sound sarcastic. "And the best part is, it's *all mine*."

"You live *alone*?" Roxy didn't know why she was so surprised; it hardly looked like anyone else lived here. "But you're only twelve. How do you live all by yourself, without a grown-up or anything?"

"'Cos I ran away. Now, where *is* that notebook?" Jones chucked a pair of tights over her shoulder. "I know I packed it."

"Jones, are you serious?" Roxy was starting to wonder if she'd bitten off more than she could chew here. Hanging out with a runaway might be exciting but it could get her into massive trouble. "You ran away from home?"

"I didn't run away from *home*. I ran away from *the house I lived in with my stepfamily*. Not the same thing at all. And it was only three days ago."

"But why?"

"Oh, I could give you a dozen reasons, if you really wanted them." Jones's face darkened. "The thing that made me decide this was *finally* it, though… Well, there was … an incident."

Roxy waited.

"A cupcake incident," Jones went on. The tip of her nose was turning pink. "I can't say any more than that. Anyway, the people here at Kettleman's know me. I've often stopped off on my delivery rounds for a *decent* baked treat to eat – not like those absurd

61

gone-in-one-bite cupcakes – so when I turned up with my suitcase the other day they told me I could crash in the attic. And with no stepmother or step-sisters bossing me around, I can do my own stuff, for the first time in my life."

"And … uh … what exactly *is* that stuff?"

"I'm a treasure hunter. I hunt for ancient artefacts of the Cursed Kingdom."

Jones was more deadly serious than ever. She didn't seem to realize how ridiculous this sounded.

"I see." (Roxy did not, in fact, see at all. But there was that mention of the *Curr-said Kingdom* again…) "So you … you've found quite a few of these … ancient artefacts, have you?"

"Nope. Not a single one. But be reasonable. I've only been doing the job full-time for a few days. Before that, it was only a hobby, so… A-ha! Got you!"

Jones pulled something from inside one of the dis-carded doughnut boxes: a small, battered notebook, made from brown leather and wrapped with a cord.

She also pulled out a large doughnut: blueberry flavour. (Either that, or it had been sitting in that box *way* too long.)

"OK, then, genius," she began, taking a bite of the doughnut.

"I never said I was a genius! This is *exactly* why

I don't tell anyone about my photographic memory! People get really weird about it."

But Jones was already pressing the notebook into Roxy's hands. "Open that at random," she said, with her mouth full, "look at a page of my notes – for ten seconds, tops – and then quote them back. *Word for word*."

"Come on, can't you just trust—?"

"I don't trust anyone."

"So you say, but you have let me up here, after all, and you've told me all ab—"

"Just do it!"

Roxy took the notebook and opened it, somewhere in the middle.

The page she had opened was covered in more of the same scribbled writing that was all over the walls. She stared at it hard, taking it all in. She was pretty sure Jones had cheated her out of a couple of seconds when the notebook was snatched away.

"Go on, then," Jones said. She was watching Roxy intently. "Do your thing. Tell me *exactly* what was written on those pages."

So Roxy did.

# MAGIC IN THE CURSED KINGDOM (THE CK)

- *Worst ratio of Dark Magic (Diabolica) to Decent Magic was in 1996, at the height of the Perpetual Wickedness: 74% to 26%.*

- *NB: See separate note on the Perpetual Wickedness; and maybe start calling it the Pep-Wick or something rather than the Perpetual Wickedness because the Perpetual Wickedness takes SO LONG to write out... Aaaaarrrrgh, there I go again.*

- *By 1997, almost half the population of the CK has fled to neighbouring countries as people try to escape rampant Dark Magic.*

- *Evil Queen Bellissima suddenly self-combusts in 1999, leaving the CK without a ruler. A year later, her third cousin, Princess Ariadne of Shiny-Newland, is finally per-suaded (by the CK's Emergency Ruling Council) to take over the job.*

- *Ariadne moves to the CK with her husband, Prince Chetwyn, is declared Queen and decides she'll have to do something pretty drastic about Diabolica or there won't be anyone left in the country for her to rule over.*

## THE GREAT CLEAN-UP (2000-2005)

- *Immediate plans to transform the kingdom begin with a purge of all Diabolical elements, e.g. a top-security*

prison is built (in the mountains?) to lock up the worst
trouble-makers.

- Main thing puzzling me about Great Clean-Up is this: how
did the regime (apparently) <u>wipe memories of every single</u>
<u>person living in the Cursed Kingdom, and every single</u>
<u>person outside it?!?!</u>

- Can't even find ONE SINGLE mention of the Cursed Kingdom
on internet except for a "spooooooooooky ghost train ride
into a Cursed Kingdom" at a massively rubbish-sounding
Family Fun Park somewhere called Aberystwyth, in Wales,
Great Britain. (NB: Never bother to visit Aberystwyth)

- Oh, and another thing: what happened to <u>Decent</u> Magic
while Dark Magic was being wiped off face of earth?
Dad's notes imply <u>all Decent Magic</u> was eliminated by new
regime too. Is this really true? (And if no magic remains
here at all, why does that little old lady sometimes show
up at the door, claiming she's collecting for a homeless-cat
charity but then as soon as she gets me on my own whispering that she's my fairy godmother(!!!) and that any time
I need help, all I have to do is wish for her???)

- NB: Try to find out if there really IS such a thing as
homeless-cat charity (even if suspicious little old lady has
absolutely nothing to do with one). And if so, make sure to
donate 10% of all future treasure-finds to them.

- OK, maybe 5%.

**7**

"Oh. My. Stars," said Jones.

She was staring at Roxy with boggling eyes and if not *exactly* a new respect then at least with the look of a person who no longer believes another person to be an utter cretin.

"You … can really do … *that*."

Roxy nodded.

"And you only looked at my notes for – what? – eight seconds."

Roxy nodded again.

"And there was no way," Jones went on, frowning, "you could possibly have seen those pages before, let alone taken the time to memorize them. Because nobody has ever seen that notebook apart from me. And you CANNOT," she added, fiercely, "talk about it to anyone. Ever. Especially the cat-charity stuff," she finished, her cheeks turning the faintest pink. "I don't need people thinking I'm soft or anything."

"Trust me," said Roxy. "I won't. I didn't even understand most of it." She swallowed, her throat suddenly feeling like sandpaper. "Jones … this *magic* thing, though…"

"Wow. Just wow." Jones's eyes were still boggling. "I have so many questions. Hey, maybe I should call you Memory Girl instead of Question Girl!"

"Please don't. And I have loads of questions too …"

"… but I can't possibly think without something to eat …"

"… so you're honestly saying that Illustria – this country – used to be this *Cursed Kingdom* place?"

"… so I'll just get changed and then we can pop downstairs and grab a Custarde Doughnut…"

"… because I've had these suspicions, about all kinds of things, really, and it's such a relief to think that maybe it's not all in my head …"

"… and you can start telling me everything you remember from *Mrs Tabitha Cattermole* …"

"… and this Diabolica thing! Is that some kind of magic? Is it *black* magic? I mean, I've never really believed in magic at all, let alone—"

"WILL YOU JUST SHUT UP FOR A BLOOMING MOMENT?" said Jones.

She was pulling off the "borrowed" tour guide uniform to reveal, underneath, khaki shorts worn over brown woolly tights, an oversized man's shirt the colour of milky coffee and belted over the hips with a wide tan belt. She still wore the same brown ankle boots on her feet.

"Right," she said, grabbing a chocolate-brown leather jacket from the pile of stuff she'd flung from the suitcase. "Let's make a deal. You're going to help me get what I need from *Mrs Tabitha Cattermole*. And in return, I'll tell you everything I know about magic. And Diabolica. And the Cursed Kingdom. Which, yes, *is* what Illustria used to be called. BUT WE'RE DOING MY THING FIRST, OK?" she added, holding up a hand to stop Roxy from interrupting. "You owe me a favour, unless I'm very much mistaken."

"OK," said Roxy meekly. "And I'm really sorry again about the whole book-burning thing. But at least now you believe that I *can* tell you everything I read in *Mrs Tabitha Cattermole*."

"Yeah. Well." Jones slung her kitbag over one shoulder. "I don't even know if there's anything useful you can tell me, yet." She stared rather hard at Roxy for a moment. "Look, I don't want to go into loads of detail. I've only just met you, after all, and I've proba-bly already told you too much. But I was sort of hoping there might have been a key in there. A map, even."

"A *key*? Inside a book?"

Jones nodded. "Just a small one, tucked inside the dust jacket, maybe."

"Jones, truly, I don't think there *was* anything hidden in there. A key *or* a map."

"Well, you might have just missed it."

"But I didn't! I promise you! I read the whole thing cover-to-cover – *twice*, by the way, even though I obviously didn't need to – and, trust me, there was absolutely nothing in there of any interest whatsoever. And I mean *nothing*." Even *thinking* about Mrs Tabitha's six hundred and fifty-two pages was enough to give Roxy a headache. "I mean, it was written in poetry, of all things."

"Yeah, well, rhyming verse is how people used to talk in the CK."

*Rhyming verse…?* Roxy thought, immediately, of that newspaper ad she'd seen. Did that have something to do with the Cursed Kingdom? If so, it made the fact it had been placed by someone calling themselves Trixie T McWitch quite a lot more intriguing…

Jones was already heading for the door. "Anyhow,

let's go and get some doughnuts – my treat – before they—"

"And come to think of it," Roxy continued, her mind racing, "there wasn't one single mention of magic in there, either. Not that I'm doubting you, Jones, but surely if there'd been a tonne of magic sloshing around the country back then, Mrs Tabitha would have said so?"

"Seriously?" Jones stopped, her hand on the door handle. "There was *no* mention of magic? At all?"

"Parsnips, yes. Magic, no."

"But that can't be true." Jones was frowning. "That book was written ages before the Great Clean-Up. It's a history of the Cursed Kingdom. She *must* have mentioned magic."

"Well, maybe it was in the missing chapter, then. Or the missing page."

*"Say that again."*

"There was a missing chapter. And a missing page. Except the missing page thing was weird," Roxy went on, "now that I think about it. I mean, even though the book suddenly jumped from Page Ten to Twelve, without a Page Eleven in the middle, it didn't seem like there were any actual *words* missing. It was more like they'd just numbered the pages wrongly, or something. And the same with the missing chapter. When

I looked at the contents page, Chapter Fifty-Three wasn't even listed. It just jumped from Chapter Fifty-Two to Chapter Fifty-Four... Jones, are you OK?"

Jones had started to hop up and down as if a family of ants had suddenly taken up residence in her pants.

"Chapter Fifty-Three was *missing*? And Page Eleven, you say?"

Roxy nodded.

"A missing chapter and a missing page! IT'S A CODE!" Jones bellowed. "An actual, real-life, blooming *code*!"

**8**

"OK, so the doughnuts are actually going to have to be *your* treat," Jones said, as they hurried down the rickety stairs towards Mrs Kettleman's, "because I'm seriously broke."

"Oh, right. Sure…"

Roxy felt hastily in her pocket for her coin purse. This was the Emergency Cash that Gretel always insisted she carried. (*For a taxi, Roxy, in case you ever end up stranded anywhere. And for an emergency meal, while you wait for the taxi, so you don't have to accept any stranger's offers of food. And for a cup of tea, so you don't get cold, and have to accept any stranger's offers of shelter.* Gretel really was a super-league worrier, with an extremely overactive imagination.)

The good news was that a plate of Twice-Glazed Caramel Custarde Doughnuts *pretty much* counted as a meal. And as Roxy hadn't eaten since her late-night snack of Proon Puffs, there was kind of an emergency element to it.

And really, the less she thought about Gretel's disapproval, the better. All the more since she was currently disobeying her sister's express order *NOT TO LEAVE THE MINISTRY GROUNDS*.

"Awesome. Been to Mrs Kettleman's before?"

"No," said Roxy. "I've not lived in Rexopolis that long. And my sister doesn't really let me have any sweet stuff."

Jones stopped at the bottom of the stairs. She looked at Roxy, aghast. "No *sweet stuff*? What is she, some kind of *dentist*, or something?"

"She's a cleaner at the Soup Ministry. I told you when we met in the vault."

"Oh, yeah." Jones was no longer looking aghast. She looked, instead, almost sympathetic. "I've cleaned a few loos in my time. It's a rotten old job."

"Well, it's not *only* loos. She cleans Minister Splendid's office. And his own *personal* loo, of course…"

"Wow," muttered Jones, with one of her eye-rolls. "Lucky lady."

The door opposite the stairs led straight into the doughnut kitchen.

"Morning, Sally. All right, there, Jimbo?" Jones

called out, as she led Roxy past half-a-dozen men and women in white chef's hats, piping various luscious-looking custards into trays of gently steaming doughnuts. "Anyone thought any more about that maple-and-sausage flavour I suggested yesterday? No takers? Oh, well. You'll all come round to the idea eventually, I know it. This way," she added, to Roxy, opening a door at the other end of the room. "Ooooh, looks like we're only just in time for the Twice-Glazed Caramels! You give me the cash and I'll order while you grab a table."

This was easier said than done.

The Emporium and Café was absolutely heaving. There were smart Ministry workers nibbling doughnuts while tapping on their phones, elegant Rexoplian ladies chatting to other elegant Rexoplian ladies over coffee and mini-doughnut bites, and even – Roxy ducked her head – a few kids lingering over a doughnut brunch when surely they should have been at school.

Thankfully, there was a tiny booth table left in the quietest corner, and Roxy scrambled into one of the seats just as Jones appeared, carrying a plate piled absurdly high with doughnuts.

"Right. Eat up, Question Girl. I need your brain firing on all cylinders."

Roxy took one of the doughnuts, which, to be fair,

did look pretty enticing: golden-hued, mirror-glazed and giving off a heavenly caramelly aroma.

"Jones," she began, timidly, "I don't mean to rain on your parade, or anything, but are you absolutely *sure* that missing page and chapter are a hidden code? Maybe it was just a mistake at the printer's?"

"Oh, QG, you're so innocent it's almost painful. Trust me, there *are* no mistakes," Jones said, grabbing a doughnut with one hand and reaching into her kitbag with the other. She pulled out the leather notebook she had used to test Roxy earlier. "And people used codes *all the time* in the CK. People practising Decent Magic who didn't want their spells or secrets falling into the hands of anyone practising Diabolica. People like Mrs Tabitha Cattermole. I have a whole section on codes somewhere in my notes... *The Hundred Years' Slumber... The Great Rapunzel Cover-Up...*" she muttered, flipping pages. "Here! *Codes and Ciphers During the Time of the Perpetual Wickedness...* Oh for heaven's sake, girl, you've just written out the entire phrase Perpetual Wickedness again when you should just have written the Pep-Wick." She waved the notebook at Roxy. "See? Right here. I've made a note on the Hide-and-Seek Code."

"Hang on. The Great *Rapunzel* Cover-Up? As in, the story about the girl with the crazy-long hair, locked in a tower by a witch?" Roxy frowned. *Witches* again. She really didn't like the frequency with which they were popping up. "But Rapunzel is only a fairytale. How could there have been a cover-up about something that never actually happened?"

"Because it did actually happen. Right here in the CK."

"*What* did you just say?"

"Rapunzel," Jones continued. "Long hair. Witch. All that stuff. It's not a fairytale in the slightest."

Roxy didn't know, really, why she should feel surprised by *anything* Jones said right now. In the last half-hour, she'd learned that magic existed; that the country she lived in used to be a different country entirely, and that for mysterious reasons great lengths had been taken to disguise this fact; that (very probably) there was a witch lurking somewhere about the place placing crazy rhyming adverts in the newspaper…

The announcement that one of her favourite childhood fairytales wasn't a *tale* at all, but had – apparently – really happened, should not have surprised her in the least.

But it had. In fact, it had done more than surprise her. For the first time in her life, Roxy thought, she knew what *flabbergasted* felt like.

"You can't be serious," she finally managed.

76

"I am. Deadly. But I'm also serious about that deal we made. Which is that I'll tell you about the CK *after* you've told me what you read in *Mrs Tabitha*." Jones rapped the table with her knuckles. "Let's focus!"

"Right…" Roxy tried to drag her mind back to what Jones wanted to discuss. "A Hide-and-Seek Code, you say?"

"Yeah. It's basically a simple book cipher." Jones took a deep breath. "Look, I'm … I'm searching for … *something*, OK? Something that's been very, very well hidden. And I believe the code for how to find this … *thing* is written in *Mrs Tabitha Cattermole's Chronicle of the Cursed Kingdom*."

She lowered her voice and leaned closer.

"To solve a code," she said, very softly, "you need a key. Right? Well, first I thought there might be an actual key in the book. But a Hide-and-Seek Code works by giving you the key *in the form of a missing chapter and a missing page*. The missing chapter number tells you the page of the book that the code is written on. In this case, *fifty-three*. And the missing page number tells you the number of words to count on that page." She lowered her voice even further. "So what we need to do is write down every *eleventh word* on *page fifty-three*, and that will crack the code."

"I get it." Roxy dropped her voice to a whisper too.

This was getting properly exciting. "So, are you going to tell me what this *thing* is you're searching for?"

Jones thought about this for a moment.

"Are you going to tell me every eleventh word on page fifty-three?"

Roxy nodded.

Jones stuck her hand over the table for Roxy to shake. "Then," she whispered, "it looks like we're partners."

Roxy's entire body was tingling, now, as if she'd been plugged into a socket.

OK, so there was the chance that Gretel was going to actually kill her.

But being Jones's partner – *whatever* that meant – was obviously ten gazillion times better than spending all day alone again.

"So, can you do your stuff?" Jones added impatiently. She was reaching for her notebook again, and producing a stubby pencil from her kitbag. "Pull your super-duper miracle-memory trick one more time?"

"OK," said Roxy. "Just give me a minute."

She closed her eyes. This was always the best way for her to "see" a book's page in her mind's eye.

"Oh!" she suddenly gasped. "Page fifty-three! That was the page that wasn't written in rhyme."

Jones's eyes glowed. "All the more reason to believe it means something."

Roxy nodded, and tried not to let the excitement get to her. She did not want to make even the tiniest mistake.

It will be of great interest, I doubt it not, for good Readers of this unworthy tome to appraise themselves of the wayes and meanes by which our subjects froze not like stone in the winter, nor baked in the summer. 'Twas not with heavy furs or thick pelts that they kept warm. Indeed, all they did use was the yarn of the sheep and the fluff combed from the Angora bunny. This gave them the power to avoid frostbite on chilly mornings. And when they did seek to remain cool in scorching August, the solution came from within the humble flax plant. With careful spinning and simple weaving, a lightweight cloth was produced, almost as if conjured from a witch's fingertips. This cloth was called linen, and it did fairly tower head and shoulders above other fabrics for maximum coolness. (I have, however, also heard good things of cotton.) In these ways, a practical yet also, for the most part, stylish and elegant look prevailed, and the Cursed Kingdom's inhabitants were the snazziest people around.

Which brings me to footwear matters. The humble boot and the simple shoe were generally favoured. The most popular and inexpensive place to purchase the above footwear was Snelling's of Hexopolis (slogan: you'll not get foul smellings with shoes from Snelling's!). One could find smart brogues, dainty slippers and the sturdiest boots, all for the most reasonable prices. Snelling's was happy to provide, too, the answer to questions of style. For example, "Do these stilettos come in fuchsia, and would they work in a formal workplace?" With your purchase also came a Snelling's carrier. Thus, with smile on face and song in heart, the Snelling's customer returned home.

53

## 9

*"For the stone with all the power, seek within a witch's tower,"* Jones read, from the notebook page on which she'd scribbled every eleventh word. *"Have a look around the place; you'll find the answer in your face."*

They were still in Mrs Kettleman's, although it had become a lot quieter since the mid-morning rush had thinned.

In fact, they were almost the only customers left, apart from a boy sitting by the window, sipping tea, his face half hidden by a lilac-coloured fedora hat. Roxy had briefly wondered why on earth a boy would be doing either of those things – tea-sipping *or* lilac-fedora-wearing – but for most of the past half-hour, she and Jones had been entirely focussed on the code.

"And you're absolutely sure it's a clue?" Roxy asked.

"Are you kidding me? It's so *obviously* a clue, it's almost embarrassing!"

"But what does it actually *mean*?" Roxy asked. "I assume *the stone with all the power* is this *thing* you said you're searching for…?"

"Might be."

"Which you're going to tell me all about at some point, right?" Roxy glanced at her new friend. "Along with telling me about Diabolica?"

"Keep your voice down!" hissed Jones. "Honestly, Question Girl, if there's one thing you should have realized by now about Diabolica –" she mouthed this word – "it's that you don't go shouting about it. Anyone could be listening!"

Roxy reddened. "Sorry. It's a lot to take in."

"Hey, I get it." Jones squeezed her, rather hard but not unkindly, on one shoulder. "My mind was blown too when I found out this stuff. And at least I learned it in little bits and bobs. It was from my dad. Well, mostly from his papers and notes, after he died last year. He was obsessed by this stuff."

"How did he know about it? I mean, it's all a huge secret, right?" Roxy glanced down at her hands, suddenly awkward. "I'm really sorry he's dead, by the way," she mumbled.

Jones shrugged in acknowledgement. "Oh, he knew

*all* about the Cursed Kingdom. I think his fairy god-mother told him about it."

"His godmother?"

"*Fairy* godmother," Jones corrected, swiping the last doughnut off the plate. "Aren't you paying attention?"

"But there's no such thing as—"

"Yeah, I have my doubts on that one too, to be honest. There's this little old lady that turns up to see me sometimes, claiming she was Dad's fairy god-mother and is now mine instead."

"Oh, the one from your notes, who says she's collecting money for depressed cats as a cover story?"

"*Homeless* cats. But I guess they'd be depressed too if they were homeless, poor little kitties…"

Roxy, however, had stopped listening.

The café doors had just opened and Bijou Splendid was strutting in.

She wasn't alone. There were two other girls with her, dressed just like Bijou in shiny tartan skater-skirts and pink hoodies, and with their hair in the same swooshy ponytails, high up on their heads and deco-rated with gigantic glittery bows.

Roxy scrunched down as far as she could in her seat, hoping Bijou didn't notice her.

"So, girls." Bijou was loudly commanding as she led the way to the largest table, in the centre of the room.

She flipped her ponytail several times, sending glitter flying. "Camera-phones at the ready, OK? When the Prince comes in for his post-tennis snack, I'm going to chat to him and I want you to video every single minute so it can go straight up on B's Buzz."

"Ohmigosh, Bijou, your fans will just *die*," gushed one of the friends.

"Like, actually properly *dead*," gushed the other, copying Bijou's ponytail-flip.

"And the Prince will, like, *so* remember you from the Queen's Ball the other night," said the first friend, copying the ponytail-flip *even harder*. "He'll be all, like, *Ohmigosh, Bijou Splendid, how's it going?* And you'll be all, like, *Ohmigosh, it's going SO well.* And he'll be, like—"

"Oi!" Jones – to Roxy's absolute horror – had turned round in her seat and was eyeballing Bijou and her friends. "Could you stop flinging your hair around, please? My doughnut's getting glitter all over it."

Bijou's eyes widened, though whether this was outrage at Jones's rudeness or the fact she'd suddenly clocked Roxy sitting there, it was impossible to tell. She definitely *had* clocked Roxy, though, because the next thing she said was, "Oh. It's *you*."

"Hi, Bijou…" Roxy had no idea what else to say. *Sorry about accidentally getting you decontaminated last night* seemed like a bad idea. "Shouldn't you be at school?"

she blurted out instead. Which was almost as bad.

"Who are you, my *teacher*?" Bijou's tiny eyes narrowed to slits.

"No, no, I just thought..."

"Do you even *remember* who my father is?" Bijou went on. "If I don't want to go to school, I don't have to go to school."

"Yes, of course," Roxy muttered. "Anyway, sorry to have disturbed you. See you around."

"Hey! We didn't disturb her! She disturbed us!" Jones hissed as Roxy busied herself looking at the notebook again. "Who *is* her father, anyway?"

"Minister Splendid," Roxy whispered back.

"The so-called Soup Minister?" Jones looked horrified. "Oh my *stars*! You could have *told* me you're friends with his daughter, before I started letting you in on all my secrets! *This* is what happens when you trust people!"

"I'm not friends with her! And you *can* trust me, Jones. One hundred per cent."

"Well, I'll just have to take your blooming word for that now, won't I?"

"And will you please explain," Roxy interrupted, "what you mean by *so-called* Soup Minister?"

"OK, QG, do you seriously still believe there needs to be an actual minister for *soup*?" Jones rolled her eyes. "Soup is literally the most uneventful thing on the planet. I'm pretty sure that's why they decided to call it the Ministry for Soup in the first place: because they knew nobody could *ever* be interested enough in soup to ask questions."

Roxy was just about to seize the moment to ask Jones what it really *was* the Ministry for, when she felt a sharp tap on her right shoulder.

It was, of course, Bijou.

"So, didn't I hear that loo-cleaner sister of yours *swear* to my father that she wouldn't be letting you out of her sight again?" Bijou folded her arms and stared down at Roxy.

"You may have heard her say … something like that…" stammered Roxy.

"Then why are you here without her? With … *this* person instead?" Bijou's top lip curled upwards as she looked at Jones. Then, clocking just how startlingly beautiful she was, the curled lip became a snarl. "Who *are* you, anyway?"

"I could ask you the same thing," said Jones.

The Bijou Clones gasped.

"I mean, I get that you're the daughter of some head honcho." Jones shrugged. "But having an important dad doesn't make you more of a big deal than the rest of us."

"Yeah?" Bijou's face was pink with fury. "I'm not *just* the daughter of the richest and most important minister in Illustria. I'm *also*, for your *information*, a MeMeMeTeeVee superstar."

"Wow," said Jones flatly. "So what's your MeMeMeTeeVee channel called, then? Is it *How to Get Glitter All Over Innocent People's Doughnuts and Generally Be a Colossal Pain in the Bum*?"

There was an ominous silence, filled only with a tiny whimper from Roxy.

"Oh. My. GOSH," gasped one of the Bijou Clones. "You can't say *bum* in this part of town. It's, like, *against the law*."

Jones's left eyebrow arched. "OK, that's literally the most stupid law I've ever heard in my life. What saddo wasted a minute of their life coming up with *that*?"

"Look," Roxy interrupted, "I'm sorry if we upset you, Bijou. We'll just leave, and—"

"We blooming *won't*! This girl doesn't get to tell us what to do!" Jones jumped up, fists clenched. "*Nobody* gets to tell me what to do any more."

"Bijou, she's, like, totally going to punch you!" screamed the second Bijou Clone.

At this, a satisfied smile spread across Bijou's face. She pulled her phone from the pocket of her hoodie.

"I'm going to call Daddy," she announced, "and tell him I've been attacked. *Then* we'll see who gets to tell people what to…"

And right at that moment, all her hair fell out.

Roxy, who'd just resigned herself to another night in that cold, frightening cell in the Decontamination Zone (or worse), could hardly believe her eyes.

But there it was: Bijou's swooshy ponytail, lying on the café's cool tiles.

"Wha- how…?" Bijou's hands went to her bald head.

Which turned, quite suddenly, into a pineapple.

Her face was now an orangey-yellow and covered in sharp, brown pineappley prickles, and at the very top of her head there was a tall stalk of rather luscious green leaves.

The Bijou Clones screamed.

Bijou screamed even louder.

Jones grabbed Roxy's arm and pulled her towards the doors.

"Come on!" she yelled. "Now!"

Roxy could hear Bijou's screams, becoming more and more outraged, as the café doors swung closed behind them.

"Faster!" Jones panted. At this precise moment, her left boot fell off, which cost them five or six heart-thumping seconds as they stopped for her to shove it back on again. "He's getting away!"

"Who's getting away?" Roxy panted back. It was news to her that they were chasing someone. "Aren't we just running away from Bijou?"

"No!" Jones was off again. "We're going after … *him*."

And with that, she *tha-wunked* her hand down onto the shoulder of the person right in front of them, a person who'd been just about to dart down the steps of Mulligatawny Square's tube station.

It was, Roxy realized as the person spun round to face them, the lilac-fedora-wearing boy who'd been sipping tea in the window seat of the café.

"What do you think you're doing?" the boy demanded.

"What are *we* doing? How about you," Jones demanded back, "and that random act of MAGIC?"

The boy let out a most un-boy-like shriek. "Don't use that word!" he gasped, flapping a hand in Roxy's direction. "She could be anyone!"

"Oh, chill out," said Jones. "Roxy's all right. She *knows*. Anyway, of course it was blooming magic, what you did back there! No one's head just randomly turns into a pineapple."

"Still, will you keep your voice down?" hissed the boy. He squirmed free from Jones's grip and darted round the side of the news stand near the tube station. "**SMOGs** all over the place today," he grumbled, "and you're running around yelling your head off about magic for all the world to hear."

"It's a bit late to be worried about that," Jones said indignantly, "when you've just turned Minister Splendid's daughter into a tropical fruit!"

"Admittedly, I wasn't really thinking. Still, at least all my spells are pre-set to wear off at the stroke of mid— Wait, what did you just say?"

"Tropical fruit?"

"Before that!"

"Minister Splendid's daughter?"

The boy's jaw dropped.

Which made it clear, for the first time, that he was wearing apricot-coloured lipstick.

"Oh, golly-golly-gosh," he whispered, taking off his hat to run a shaking hand through his hair.

Which made it clear, for the first time, that he was also wearing moss-green eyeshadow, thick black mascara and a pearly-peach blusher.

"Silly mistake of mine this morning," he muttered, seeing Roxy and Jones's startled faces, "putting on my usual make-up without thinking. I only realized when I saw my face in the back of a teaspoon back there. Good thing I had a hat in my handbag." He waggled the bag he was carrying, which – now Roxy saw – actually *was* a handbag, a huge shoulder bag in daffodil-yellow leather. "Now, are you *absolutely sure* that was Minister Splendid's daughter?"

"Positive," said Roxy, finding her voice at last.

The boy let out a high-pitched wail. "And all I was trying to do was stand up for my goddaughter!"

"I'm not your goddaughter," said Roxy. "I don't even have a godfather." (Let alone, she would have added if she knew a polite way to say it, one who was ten years old.)

"Not you, dear!" The boy pointed at Jones. *"Her!* I've been keeping my *godmotherly* eye on her since she ran away from home."

"But I don't have a…" Jones stopped. "Wait a minute," she said. "You're not … *Frankie*?"

The boy nodded, and gave a little curtsy. "The very same. Your one and only fairy godmother!"

**10**

"Wow," said Jones in an awed voice. "I mean … just … wow. Last time I saw you, you were a little old lady, pretending to collect money for homeless cats."

"I *am* a little old lady!" said the boy indignantly. "I just tried this new Miracle Makeover spell on myself and it went rather badly wrong. It was supposed to make me look as radiant as I was in my two-hundred-and-sixties. I'm still not sure how it turned me into a ten-year-old. And a *boy*. And it's taking longer to wear off than usual. Honestly, my spells never usually last past midnight, but this one's lingering and lingering…"

"This is the most awesome news!" Jones let out a little whoop and pulled Frankie in for a hug. "Your timing could not be better! Roxy and I could really use a BOBI right now."

"Bobby?" Roxy stared at Jones. "He said his name was *Frankie*."

Jones gave a hoot of laughter. "Not B-O-B-B-Y. Frankie *is* a BOBI. B-O-B-I."

"It stands for Being of Benign Intent, dear," Frankie said, squeezing Roxy's hand with his own, faintly powdery one. "BOBI is the name for the Decent Magical people that are still allowed to live in this country. Under strict regulations, that is. And in total secrecy. Both of which I've just entirely disregarded," he sighed, "by zapping the Minister's daughter, of all people."

"Oh, don't stress about that," said Jones. "She probs won't even tell anyone about it. Too embarrassing."

"That's not the point!" Frankie was actually wringing his hands now. "Such a silly, thoughtless thing for me to do! Performing unauthorized magic is more foolhardy than ever, what with all the extra **SMOG** patrols around these past couple of days. Granted, they've got bigger fish to fry today – they won't be worrying about one teensy-weensy little transformation spell – but even so…"

"What fish," Jones demanded, "have they got to fry?" Her ears seemed to have almost pricked up, like a dog's. "Is something going on?"

"Oh, well, dearie, I shouldn't be talking about it to

non-BOBIs, I really shouldn't…" Frankie looked torn for a moment, but it was all too evident that he liked a bit of a gossip. "There's been a *breakout*," he mouthed dramatically, "from a top-security Dark Magic prison."

"Whoa!" Jones let out a whistle. "You mean the one in the mountains, where all the Diabolical prisoners are kept?"

"That's the one. There are only rumours at the moment, of course, about *which* prisoner has escaped. But when you *think* about the dreadful characters that have been kept there…" Frankie shuddered. "I was on my way this morning to find out what my dear friend Diadora might know about it – she's a witch, after all, a *good* witch of course, but still, she'll be more up to date with the underground news than any of my fairy friends – when the itching in my earlobes got even worse. So obviously I had to deal with that first."

"Itching in your earlobes?" Roxy asked anxiously. "Is that anything to do with this Diabolical breakout?"

"Oh, no, dearie! That's a fairy godmother thing." Frankie squeezed Roxy's hand again. "Our earlobes itch when our godchildren are in danger. And thank *goodness* that they do!" he added severely to Jones. "After all, how else would I know what's going on with my only goddaughter? You didn't even *try* to wish for me to come, not once! Not even after I came to check up on you, pretending to be that ridiculous home-less-cat charity collector! How was I to know things had got *that* bad at home? Our earlobes only itch when you're in danger, not when you're plain miserable."

"It's true," said Jones, unusually meek. She was, Roxy realized, Up To Something. "You're right, Frankie, and I feel bad about it. But better late than never, right?"

"I suppose..." began Frankie suspiciously.

"So, this witch friend you said you were going to visit... Any chance Roxy and I could tag along?"

"Oh! My dear! BOBIs and non-BOBIs aren't sup-posed to fraternize these days. Why do you think I pretended to be that homeless-cat loon? Anyway, what could you possibly need to meet a witch for?"

"Well, we're on a bit of a ... well, let's call it a scav-enger hunt. Just for fun, really. Looking for a witch's tower, as it happens. I thought a proper witch might be able to point us in the right direction."

"*Scavenger hunt?*" Frankie looked alarmed. "Is it *dangerous*? Oh, what am I saying – of *course* it's danger-ous to go looking for a witch's tower, two non-BOBIs like you! All these **SMOGs** around at the moment, you could get into the most terrible trouble!"

"We'll wait before we actually go to the witch's tower, then," Jones said, pressing her foot hard on

Roxy's, which almost certainly meant she was fibbing and didn't want Roxy to say so. "Let this whole break-out thing die down first. But *please*, Frankie, let us come with you. After all," she wheedled, "you're my fairy godmother. You're *supposed* to help me when I need you, right?"

"True, dear, but that's more in situations where – oh, I don't know – you might need my help getting to a fancy ball…"

Jones snorted.

"… or when you want to meet a handsome prince…"

Jones made a retching noise.

"Oh, fine!" snapped Frankie. "I suppose the **SMOGs** have bigger things to worry about today than a bit of illegal fraternizing. Besides, the **SMOG** patrols tend to leave Sector Seven to itself."

"Sector Seven? That's where we're going?" Jones let out a little whoop of excitement. "Where all the BOBIs live?"

"Not *all* of them, dear. But it's where Diadora lives." Frankie put his hat back on. "Hmm. It's quite a walk. Although, I did buy all that veg in the supermarket earlier…"

He delved deep into the yellow handbag and, a moment later, pulled out a cauliflower and a very shiny purple aubergine.

Jones and Roxy stared down at them.

"How are a couple of vegetables," Jones asked, finally, "supposed to get us to the other side of town?"

"Oh, dear child, Vegetable Vehicles are the *hottest* thing in fairy magic right now. All my friends are transforming vegetables like crazy!" Frankie shot a quick glance over his shoulder to check no one was listening in. "Cabbages into bicycles, onions into milk floats… D'you know, at brunch with the girls last Saturday, I managed to transform an avocado into a scooter. I was ever so chuffed!" Frankie delved back into the bag and pulled out a small pumpkin. "Now, this would take *really* advanced magic. But I was thinking of giving it a go sometime—"

"I'm allergic to pumpkin," Jones interrupted. "But if you can seriously make something out of that aubergine – her eyes were glittering with excitement – "that would be *ep*—"

"Absolutely not." Roxy spoke firmly, surprising herself almost as much as them. "You said it yourself, Frankie, **SMOGs** are everywhere at the moment. And I've already been decontaminated once!"

"You're quite right, dear." Nodding vigorously, Frankie slipped the vegetables back into his handbag. "I don't know what came over me. Let's just hop on the tube! It's only three stops if we take the Splendid line.

That's by far the most sensible way to get to Sector Seven."

They took the tube.

Jones was in a total sulk about it, refusing to even sit next to Roxy and, instead, sprawling across an entire row opposite, listening to Roxy's music on Roxy's phone through Roxy's headphones. (Her sulk didn't extend to refusing this generous offer.)

"Well, this is nice, isn't it, dear?" Frankie was making himself comfortable in the seat beside Roxy. Fortunately, they had the carriage to themselves. He reached into his handbag and pulled out a bag of jelly sweets. "You look like you could use one of these!"

"Thank you." Roxy took an orange sweet and popped it into her mouth, relishing the sugary hit. She sat back in her seat and closed her eyes for a moment. "Everything's been a bit of a surprise, to be honest."

"Yes, it's quite the shock for the few who ever find out!" Frankie nodded with great satisfaction. "Us BOBIs operate in total secrecy, you see. That's the condition under which we're allowed to stay in Illustria. The so-called Soup Minister is very clear about that."

This – finally – was the chance for Roxy to have her question answered.

"Look, I've been dying to know. If the Soup Ministry isn't actually anything to do with soup, what's it the Ministry *for*?"

"Moo," said Frankie.

This was disconcerting, to say the least.

"Spelled like this," Frankie added, reaching into his handbag for a biro and writing on Roxy's hand.

Roxy glanced down and read the word *MOOOOOH*.

"It stands," Frankie said, "for Ministry Overseeing, Organizing Or Occasionally Opposing Hocus-Pocus."

"That's a completely bonkers name," said Roxy.

"Can't argue with that, dearie!"

Roxy could only imagine what Gretel would say if she ever found out any of this stuff.

"So it's really a kind of ... magic-control ministry?"

Frankie nodded. "The high-ups are big on *control*. And trust me, dear, there's a lot more than just the *occasional* opposing of hocus-pocus. Mind you, they needed control when they first took over. This place was chock-full of all those horrible Diabolica-worshippers; it was giving magic a bad name."

"But why do you stay?" Roxy couldn't help asking. "If you're not allowed to be yourselves apart from behind closed doors?"

"Because it's our home, dear child, just as much as it is yours. You're from Illustria, I presume?"

"Yes. At least, I was born here, but I've moved around over the years." Roxy knew she was rambling, but this time it wasn't from nerves. There was something so grandmotherly about the sweet-faced boy sitting beside her that she wanted to tell him everything. "My dad gets married quite a lot. We usually move to wherever my new stepmum lives. And at the last count, I've had, I think, ten stepmothers. Or maybe it's eleven. I lose track. *And* Dad was married four times before I even came along. My own mum was my half-brother and half-sister's *third* stepmum."

"You poor darling!" Frankie proffered another fruit jelly. "And your own mother is dead, of course?"

"Oh, no. Mum's alive and well. At least, I *think* she's alive and well. I only get the occasional message since she left my dad and set off to 'find herself' eight years ago. The last time I heard from her she was in India. Or maybe it was Nepal. I hope she's finding herself better than I'm finding *her*, that's all I can say!"

"Goodness." Frankie's eyes, beneath the brim of his lilac fedora, were bulging. "How ... modern! Of course –" he nodded at Jones across the aisle – "my poor goddaughter had a *lovely* mother herself, rest her soul. Not like that vile stepmother, threatening to call the police because of one tiny cupcake incident."

*"She got that waaaaaaaart,"* Jones suddenly sang

out, in a voice like a corncrake with laryngitis, *"on the eeeeeend of her noh-oh-oh-OHSE*. You know –" mercifully, she had stopped singing – "I quite like this H-Bomb and the Missiles stuff. I mean, yeah, it's miserable. And weirdly obsessed with witches. But you forget how that H-Bomb guy can really *sing*."

"Well, at least *someone* can," said Frankie crisply, getting to his feet as the tube pulled into a station. "Pleasant Street! This is our stop, my dears! Follow me!"

Obediently, the girls followed Frankie off the train, up the escalator and out of the station.

"I can't believe it's actually here." Jones was gazing around, in open awe, as they came out into the fresh air. "I've only been to Pleasant Street Station once before. I delivered two dozen red-velvet cupcakes to an office near by. I never knew Sector Seven was here!"

"You have to know exactly where you're going," said Frankie, bustling down the busy shopping street before taking a sharp right at a smaller, rather less swanky branch of Mrs Kettleman's Doughnuts. The road they found themselves on was already quieter than the main one, and noticeably more shabby. "It's exactly seven paces along here," Frankie continued, measuring out the seven paces before taking a left turn, "and then we'll take the seventh turning to the left. We magical folk do love a nice seven!" Jones's fairy godmother cast an eye around as they hurried along the street. "It's been months since I was here. It's more run-down than ever!"

Roxy silently agreed. This was certainly not the picture-perfect Rexopolis the tourists got to see. The street they were taking now was narrow, and flanked by high, grey blocks of flats with not enough windows. The few shops – a minimart here, a phone store there – had dusty windows and looked thin on both stock and customers.

"Basically, after the Great Clean-Up, Minister Splendid built all these mega-grim flats," Jones explained, seeing Roxy's face, "and forced all the BOBIs to live here so he could keep tabs on them."

"Don't be so dramatic, dear." Frankie tutted. "Nobody is *forced* to live here. They're more kind of … encouraged. And yes, Minister Splendid did build all these rather spartan flats for them to live in. But really, if you'd seen some of the grotty hovels inhabited by the elven folk back in the Cursed Kingdom—"

"So why don't *you* live here, then?" Jones asked, not-terribly-politely.

"I just prefer to live among regular people. Ooooh, you two must come for tea at my flat one day, when the **SMOG** patrols have died down a bit. It's only small, but, my dears, the city views are to die for!"

Just as Frankie said this, they came out, abruptly, into a kind of square – though technically it was a septagon rather than a square, as it had seven distinct sides.

"This is the Septagon," said Frankie (which made a lot of sense). "The heart of Sector Seven."

It didn't look like a very healthy heart. It was almost entirely deserted apart from a couple of shabby market stalls and a pavement café with half a dozen customers, three of whom got up and left their seats the moment Frankie, Jones and Roxy walked into the Septagon.

"Rude!" muttered Frankie. "Honestly, this is why I don't socialize with many BOBIs these days. They're so skittish around strangers! Now, let's head down Street Seven Point Five –" he began to cross the Septagon – "and head to dear Diadora's flat."

"Diadora is a nice name," said Roxy politely.

"Oh, yes, isn't it? It's a fairy name, traditionally. But then, although Diadora is a witch, her mother was a fairy. One of Sleeping Beauty's fairy godmothers, in fact." Frankie shot a side-eyed glance at Jones. "*Some* lucky fairies get lovely, *easy* godchildren."

"Load of pig poo," said Jones, not looking the slightest put out. "It's easy to be easy if you drop off for a hundred years."

"Anyway, Diadora's mother, Daphne the Dandelion Fairy, is the clever one who managed to weaken the evil fairy Mortadella's curse, so Sleeping Beauty was only put to sleep, instead of dying."

"So it's not just Rapunzel?" Roxy glanced from Jones to Frankie and back again. "It's Sleeping Beauty, too?"

"It's *all* the fairytales, OK?" Jones said, waving a laconic hand. "They're all true. They all really happened. Every single—"

She was interrupted by the roar of an engine, followed by the screech of brakes.

A midnight-blue **SMOG** van had hurtled into the Septagon and stopped right outside the pavement café. A moment later, the van doors were thrown open.

"**SMOG** patrol!" gasped Frankie. "We're doomed!"

## 11

Frankie grabbed both girls by the elbow and yanked them down the nearest side street.

Roxy almost lost her footing. "What are you—"

"Oh, do hush, dearie!" Frankie was pressed against the wall of one of the houses that lined Seven Point Three Street, sweating beneath his face powder. "We mustn't be seen!"

"That's one *massive* **SMOG** patrol. And they're heavily armed, too!" Jones peeked back round the corner, ignoring Frankie's squeak. "Those IPLs are pretty awesome. D'you know, I think they're actually carrying two each?"

"What do you think they're doing?" Roxy asked nervously. "Is this anything to do with that prison breakout?"

"Of course!" Frankie was white-faced beneath his

make-up and looked as if he might happily double over and vomit on the cobblestones. "I'll bet it's a random licence check! That's the only reason the **SMOGs** ever come to Sector Seven. They must have ordered one because of the breakout!"

"Licence check?" echoed Roxy. "What does that mean?"

"All BOBIs have to have a licence if they want to stay in Illustria," muttered Jones, who was still watching the Septagon. "MOOOOOH gives them out, right, Frankie? And you have to have it renewed every five years? Oh, wow, here come even more of them!" she added as a second vehicle came roaring into the Septagon. This time, Roxy could see, it was a midnight-blue car: an extremely sleek and shiny one. A uniformed driver got out of the front and opened the back door for the passenger.

The person who climbed out was a small woman with grey hair and glasses, dressed in grey trousers and a grey parka. She wore a pleasant smile, and carried a rolled-up black umbrella.

"It's Mrs Smith," croaked Frankie.

*Mrs Smith.* Roxy's ears pricked up at the name. Minister Splendid had mentioned her. *This was the person Gretel had said did not exist.*

Frankie was now backing away down Seven

Point Three Street. His eyes were fixed on Mrs Smith, out in the Septagon. "D'you know, dear hearts, I don't think I'll be able to take you to meet Diadora after all."

"Hey! You said you'd help us!" Jones pointed an accusing finger. "What's going on? I mean, OK, I'll admit, **SMOGs** are a bit intimidating, but why all the panic about this Mrs Smith person? Who even *is* she?"

"No panic, dearie, no panic!" said Frankie with a slightly strained laugh. "I'm perfectly, perfectly at ease around Mrs Smith! Or, as we all *used* to know her in the olden days, Wincey the Wisteria Fairy."

"Don't tell me. Another one of Sleeping Beauty's lucky fairy godmothers?"

"Yes, dear. And now she works for Minister Splendid. She's his deputy, actually." Frankie took a deep breath. "And the thing is ... if it *is* a random licence-check ... well, I'm not *one hundred per cent* certain, but my own licence may be ... ah ... just a teensy-weensy bit out of date."

"How out of date?" Roxy asked.

"Erm ... well, gosh, now, let me see... It's been, ooooh, a good twenty years since the Great Clean-Up ... so that would make my licence ... ummm ... well, OK, I may not ever have actually got one."

He mumbled this last part so quietly that Roxy

wasn't sure they'd heard him right.

"You never got one?" demanded Jones.

"Not as such, dearie," Frankie mumbled, "no."

Both girls stared at him.

"Look, getting a licence can be *hard*!" said Frankie plaintively. "MOOOOOH has files, and video footage, and they interrogate you for two or three days straight. And, well, I may have occasionally hung out with the wrong sort of people in my much younger days. No *bad*-magic elements – never! – but a few of what you might call *naughty*-magic elements. I was a … a rather wild young fairy, I'm ashamed to say."

"That's why you don't live here in Sector Seven, isn't it?" demanded Jones. "Because MOOOOOH keep more of an eye on people who live here—"

"If we get caught while we're with you," Roxy interrupted as an image of Gretel's shocked – no, *devastated* – face popped into her mind, "and you're unlicensed, will that get us into even bigger trouble?"

Before Frankie could answer, a booming voice came from the Septagon.

"SECTOR SEVEN INHABITANTS." The voice belonged to the **SMOG** captain, who was holding a megaphone. "PAY ATTENTION. THERE HAS BEEN A SECURITY BREACH."

"They *are* here because of the breakout!" hissed

Frankie. "I should have known it was a bad day to come! Oh, Frankie, you silly, *silly* fairy!"

"WE ARE ABOUT TO CONDUCT A RANDOM SEARCH OF THE AREA," came the **SMOG** captain's voice again. "PLEASE PRESENT YOUR LICENCE AND IDENTIFICATION PAPERS WHEN ASKED TO DO SO."

"We have to get out of Sector Seven," gurgled Frankie. *"Now."*

"DO NOT ATTEMPT TO LEAVE SECTOR SEVEN," boomed the voice. "ALL EXITS ARE SEALED."

"What are we going to do?" Roxy's heart was thudding. Out in the Septagon, she could see that Mrs Smith, with the same pleasant smile on her face, was taking the megaphone from the captain.

"This is Mrs Smith speaking," she said, her voice crisp and clear. "I would like to assure my fellow BOBIs that there is no reason to be alarmed. The usual procedures will be followed. Law-abiding folk need have no fear."

"Which would be reassuring," hissed Jones, "if we were actually *with* a law-abiding BOBI."

"Oh, for heaven's sake, child, just let me *think* a minute!" said Frankie. "We're on Seven Point Three Street, am I right?"

"Yes."

"Then we can make it to my friend Skinny's instead! It's much closer, and we'll be safe there. Come on, dearies!" Frankie set off at a rather bouncy, arm-flapping trot. The street continued to wind away from the Septagon, narrowing as it went, and they'd been jogging steadily for several minutes when Frankie began to slow down. "Number Seven-Eight-Four... Number Seven-Eight-Six... We're here!"

They'd stopped outside a grimy shop window. A sign above said: **BOGIE WONDERLAND.**

"Frankie," began Jones, "why have you brought us to a shop that sells *bogeys*?"

"It's supposed to say *Boogie*," Frankie sighed. "As in, *dancing to good music*. Not as in, *the contents of your nostrils*. I have *told* him about his appalling spelling. Numerous times." He pushed open the front door.

The shop inside was piled, from floor to ceiling, with something that Roxy instantly recognized: old vinyl records, the kind people used to play music on creaky old record players, in the days before instant digital downloads.

It was, at a swift glance, almost as impressive a collection as the one belonging to her brother.

"Oh, wow," Roxy breathed, forgetting to NOT act like a total music geek. She stepped forward, reading aloud from some of the covers she could see in the nearest pile. "*Patagonia Dreaming* by Electric Funk Suitcase... *Hell on Four Wheels* by Zadie Starburst... This is incredible!"

"Excuse me," interrupted a voice from behind the pile of records. "That's my beard you're trampling on."

Roxy glanced down to see that she was definitely standing on *something*.

It was, indeed, a beard. It was a very, very long beard. It was wispy, and faintly gingery, and it belonged to the very, very short man who now appeared from behind the stack of records.

**12**

The bearded man was wearing baggy cargo shorts, and sunglasses, and a crumpled T-shirt with the words SMELLS LIKE TEEN SPIRIT printed on it. He was holding a plank of wood and, alarmingly, a large hammer. He was not smiling.

"I'm s-sorry," Roxy stammered. "I didn't see you there … or your beard."

"Skinny, dear," said Frankie, stepping towards him. "It's me."

"Frankie?" The little man dropped the plank of wood. "What the blooming heck's happened to you?"

"Oh, just a bad makeover spell, dearie. Now, look, there's a random licence-check going on out there…"

"And you never got round to actually applying for your licence, so you want to hide out here." Skinny, behind his sunglasses, was still not smiling. He didn't seem the sort of person to take kindly to unexpected visitors (and it was not merely the hammer that was giving this impression). "I'm honoured."

"Now, don't be grumpy, Skinny. I was actually bringing my friends to meet you, too!" Frankie was quite clearly making this up on the spot. "They have a few questions about witches, as it happens, and I suspect you're just the chap to help them out."

Skinny waved the hammer in sudden alarm. "What's *wrong* with you, woman? Or *boy*. Or whatever," he hissed. "Today, of *all* days, you stand here in my store and talk about *witches*?"

"But I'm talking about *good* witches, dear…"

"It doesn't matter *which* witches you're talking about! If the **SMOGs** hear talk of *any* witches, we'll all be carted off faster than you can say, *Guess who's broken out of the so-called top-security prison for Diabolicals*."

"Oh, my days." Frankie gazed at him. "Is it as bad as all that?"

"Yep."

"It's … *her*, isn't it?"

"Yep again."

Frankie's eyes widened so far that his pupils were scarcely visible in the surrounding white. "Do you know, dear," he murmured, "I suddenly feel very much in need of a cup of hot, sweet tea."

"You know where the kettle is," Skinny grunted. Then, as Frankie bustled past him towards the back of the store, he turned his attention to the two girls. "So," he snapped, "are you all right?"

Roxy was just about to stammer that she was very well, thank you, when Jones nudged her sharply in the ribs.

"Yeah," she said, tilting her chin. "We're *all right*."

This, Roxy realized, must be a way of letting BOBIs know that you knew about them and their magical powers, and that you would keep it all a secret.

"So let me guess which of the seriously scary Marys has broken out," Jones went on, leaning casually on a pile of records. "The Gingerbread Witch? Baba Yaga? Or— Aaaaaaaaaarghhh!"

The pile of records had toppled to the floor, Jones beneath them.

"Careful!" shrieked Skinny, darting forward. "What's wrong with you, girl? Those are priceless records you're vandalizing! There's a *Candypain: The Live Sessions* by H-Bomb and the Missiles right there, under your bum! Do you have any idea how rare that disc is?"

Roxy had been about to help Jones up from the dusty floor, but she stopped in surprise. "You like H-Bomb?"

"I don't *like* H-Bomb. I *love* H-Bomb." Skinny's eyes narrowed. "Why? Do *you*?"

"Yes! I've got *Candypain: The Live Sessions* too! I mean, not as an actual record, but it's on my phone."

"You're joking me." Skinny's angry, creased little face was unfurling like a flower towards the sun. "I thought girls like you only listened to cheeseballs like Spencer Sick-Bucket, or whatever his name is. How did you get into *Candypain: The Live Sessions*?"

"It's a long story. But it's one of my favourite H-Bomb albums."

"Mine too! I mean, don't get me wrong, I love their later stuff, but back in those early days…"

"OK, there's really no time for the music-nerd chit-chat." Jones, pink in the cheeks from embarrassment, was struggling to her feet by herself. "First off, can we please be clear on one thing: you're Rumpelstiltskin, right?"

Skinny's face swiftly shut down again. "What? Who? Never heard of him."

And with that, he began to stomp towards the door at the back of the store.

"Oh, come on! You're the spitting image." Jones scurried after him and Roxy reluctantly left the records to follow. After all, if Jones was right, this was a face-to-face encounter with an actual fairy tale person! Roxy's head might be spinning with what she'd only recently learned about fairytales, but meeting Rumpelstiltskin *in the flesh* was too extraordinary a moment to miss. "The beard," Jones went on, "the slightly bad mood ... and don't tell me those delicate hands of yours aren't made for spinning straw into gold!"

This made Skinny spin round, both fists (which were, indeed, Roxy now saw, surprisingly delicate for such a stocky man) raised. "I swear, if *anyone* mentions straw..."

"OK, calm down. I'm sorry," said Jones, sounding genuinely contrite in the face of such instant fury. "I won't say the S-word again."

"You'd better not." Stomping even harder now, Skinny led them into the back room, where a badly shaken Frankie was putting four chipped mugs on a fold-out table while a kettle boiled behind him.

It was impossible to work out, Roxy thought, whether this was a stockroom or where Skinny in fact lived. There were more records piled up everywhere but there was also a slouchy leather armchair half-covered with a crocheted blanket, some ropey old striped curtains, an ancient microwave and – visible through another little doorway – a small shower-room with a rickety loo. The back door had been half boarded up: clearly they really had interrupted Skinny right in the middle of doing it.

"Anyway, Rumpelstiltskin was just a fairytale!" Skinny seemed unable to let Jones's comments go. He stuffed his hands into his pockets. "A made-up, totally fictional *story*. Nonsense for children. Imaginary. Make-believe. A folderol. A—"

"Yeah, look, we know fairytales are actually real," said Jones. "So that won't wash with us. And come on, you're here boarding up your door because some so-called fairytale witch – oh, and I'm guessing it's Queen Bellissima, by the way – has escaped from prison. That sounds pretty real to me."

"You know the truth about fairytales?" Skinny looked astonished. "But what … how…? Has the False Memory Enchantment failed, or something?"

"The Enchantment is just fine," said Frankie. "It's my fault, I'm afraid, that my goddaughter knows about us. I may have chatted a wee bit too freely to her father when he was a boy."

"Ooooh, I've never *heard* of the False Memory Enchantment." Jones was already reaching into her kitbag for her notebook. "What is it?"

"It's an APPALLING PIECE OF SKULDUGGERY AND DECEIT!" bellowed Skinny, bashing a furious (tiny) fist on the table so hard that the mugs jumped. It was easy to see how they'd become so chipped.

"Skinny, do try to stay calm, dear. We have quite enough to get stressed about already. And I'm painfully aware," Frankie went on, to Jones, "that you'll badger me about it until I lose the will to live, so I'll explain." He set down the steaming teapot, sat down heavily on the armchair and sighed. "The False Memory Enchantment is the most powerful spell that's ever existed, and – probably – ever will exist. It keeps everybody in Illustria under the illusion that fairytales are just fiction, rather than actual history."

"Not only in Illustria!" sputtered Skinny. "The magic used for the Enchantment is channelled through the Witching Stones. That makes it powerful enough to keep it operating over the *entire world*!"

"Skinny!" Frankie squawked, horrified. "You can't tell them about the Stones!"

"Why not? Apparently you've told them pretty much everything else."

"But Skinny, the *Stones* … they're top secret! Topper than top! They're … oh, well, it's too late now, I suppose," sighed Frankie, starting to pour the tea with an air of resignation. "They may as well know now. If *she's* escaped, the entire world as they know it could be over by next week anyway."

"Really?" Roxy asked, sharply. In truth, she was a lot more interested in finding out more about this terrifying escaped prisoner than in hearing about these magical stones: surely the escapee was the number-one priority right now. But evidently Jones didn't feel the same.

"So, this Stone," she said casually, beginning to scribble in her notebook. "Tell me more."

"Stones," said Skinny. "Plural. There are seven of them."

"*Seven?*" Jones's head snapped up. "I thought there was onl…" She stopped abruptly. "How interesting," she went on, burying her head in her notebook again. "Do carry on."

*Now* Roxy was paying attention.

There was something about the oh-so-innocent angle of Jones's head as she scribbled – not to mention what she'd just blurted out – that had totally, massively, without-a-shadow-of-a-doubt given it away.

These Witching Stones were the *thing* she was looking for.

Or rather, as Jones had clearly thought there was only one, *a* Witching Stone.

"They're rare magical stones that contain so much power themselves, they magnify any spell you perform when in contact with one," Skinny went on.

"So if any old non-BOBI chanted one while holding a Stone, it would make that spell so powerful that they could, I dunno, turn their nasty Great-Uncle Nigel into a Parmesan cheese, or make their least-favourite teacher's nose turn blue."

"Oh, *really*?" said Roxy, looking rather pointedly at Jones. "So they could be used to harm people you're angry with, for example? Like, family members?" She paused before adding, *"Stepmothers?"*

Jones was deliberately ignoring the pointed look. In fact, to aid her in ignoring it *completely*, she picked up Frankie's lilac fedora from where he'd left it on the table and popped it on her head at an angle that almost completely shielded her eyes. "Interesting stuff," she said to Skinny, way too casually. "Fascinating piece of brand-new information."

"And there aren't seven, actually," added Frankie. "There are six. They're the ones that, jointly, channel the False Memory Enchantment. Nobody even knows if the *Seventh* Witching Stone still exists. It's almost certain it was found – and then quickly destroyed – during the Great Clean-Up. It was by far the most powerful Stone, you see, and the only one that could channel Dark Magic as well as Decent Magic."

"Course it still exists, woman!" Skinny threw up his hands, sloshing tea over the armchair. "Why else do you think Bellissima has broken out of prison?"

"Ha! So it *is* her!" Jones punched a triumphant fist. "I was right!"

"Congratulations, dear," said Frankie dryly. "Anyway, *she* knows the Seventh Stone is still out there. And remember – she's only a spirit these days, no more than a puff of smoke. She'll know there's only one thing powerful enough to rebuild a body, and that's the Seventh Stone!"

"She's … sorry, this Bellissima is a *puff of smoke*?" Roxy had to ask.

"Oh, yes, dear," said Frankie. "The truth is right there, in the fairytale: Snow White's stepmother, Queen Bellissima, went up in a furious puff of smoke, remember, when she found out Snow White hadn't been killed by her poisoned apple?"

"Although how Splendid's people managed to *capture* a puff of smoke, and then lock it up, is a mystery to me!" said Skinny. "But trust me, that evil spirit will be wafting around out there right now, knowing that she'll never get her full strength back without that Stone. And when she does, trust me, we'll all be back to the darkest days of the Perpetual Wickedness."

"Skinny! Please! There's no need to frighten the children!"

"Hey, I'm not frightened," breathed Jones. "This is *awesome*! So just out of interest, do you think this Seventh Witching Stone could be described as … uh … *the stone with all the power*?"

Skinny snorted. "Well, it magnifies any spell by thousands and thousands and thousands. So even a totally non-magical non-BOBI like you would be able to cast a pretty decent one. Imagine that power in the hands of a magical being who can already cast dizzyingly potent spells all on their own. Now imagine that power in the hands of someone who practises *Dark Magic*…"

Roxy, who *was* pretty frightened by now, cleared her throat.

"So it really doesn't sound great that Queen Bellissima's the one who escaped. I mean, if she's half as bad as the fairytale says, she's pretty much as nasty as they come."

"Obviously you can debate that," said Skinny abruptly, "if you *want* to give yourself nightmares. Was she the worst Dark Magic practitioner of all, or was it the Gingerbread Witch? Take your pick, really. For me, it's *her*. Bellissima. No contest."

Frankie reached out a hand and squeezed his old friend's shoulder. "The thing is," he said, "you sweet, innocent girls couldn't possibly understand how bad things were in the late days of the Cursed Kingdom. None of the Dark Magic that had come before had anything on the Old Queen's evil power. She could do anything, *anything at all*, and there wasn't a magical being alive powerful enough to stop her."

"She'd slaughter people just for the fun of it," Skinny went on. "Wipe out whole villages – towns, even. On a whim! You might head off to buy a prawn sandwich and an apricot flapjack one lunchtime and come home to find your house a smouldering ruin, burned to the ground by the queen's purple fire, with everything you loved still inside. Your records. Your hamsters. Your only sister."

"Now, Skinny." Frankie spoke softly. "What do we always say, dear? Better not to speak of it. Better not to remember."

There was a short silence. Frankie stared into space. Skinny stared into his milky tea. Roxy, not knowing quite *where* to look, stared down at her feet. And Jones stared pointedly at Roxy.

"Can I have a quick word with you, Roxy?" she asked. "In private?"

Roxy hesitated. After hearing that outburst from Skinny, she had to say something. She just didn't have a clue *what*. "Skinny, I'm so, so…"

"Give Skinny a moment to himself, perhaps…"

Jones grabbed Roxy's arm and pulled her back through the door to the musty record store. "Oh. My. Stars. This is HUGE!" she hissed, closing the door behind her.

"The fact that poor Skinny's sister – and his hamsters – were murdered by an evil witch whose spirit is now on the run from prison?" Roxy was feeling sick. "Jones, come on. I don't know if *huge* is how I'd describe it."

"No, well, that's obviously massively tragic." Jones, in fairness, did look a bit sick about this herself. She even took off the fedora that she was still wearing, in an apparent show of respect for the dead. "But what's the use in us all sitting around feeling sad about it when there's actually something we can *do*?"

"About Skinny's dead sister?"

"To stop anything awful like that happening again!" Jones's eyes were glittering like a pair of electrified sapphires. "*Think* about it, QG! We're already on the trail of this Seventh Witching Stone, right?"

"If it's *the stone with all the power* from Mrs Tabitha's clue, then yes, we are. And honestly, *were* you searching for it to get revenge on your stepmother?"

"Well, yeah, OK, a bit. Well, maybe a lot. But also because it's *the* biggest historical artefact from the Cursed Kingdom! You heard them in there!"

"I also heard Frankie say that MOOOOOH probably found it *and destroyed it*, Jones. I mean, remember how quickly they destroyed *Mrs Tabitha*, as soon as they discovered it?"

"Load of pig poo!" scoffed Jones. "I bet they'd been looking for that book for years, with absolutely no idea it had been stuffed away right under their noses in a dusty old storage vault! And I bet they haven't really burnt it, and that teams of crack MOOOOOH codebreakers are working on that clue even as we speak."

"Um, well then, shouldn't we just let them get on with it? I mean, they are the ones in charge, Jones. If Skinny's right, and Queen Bellissima is trying to find the Seventh Stone, it has to be found, and by the right people, as fast as possible."

"Exactly! But who says Minister Splendid and his agents are the right people?" Jones gestured the fedora wildly in the (very rough) general direction of central Rexopolis and the Soup Ministry. "What makes you think we could trust them with the Stone? If they've used the six less powerful ones to cast some dishonest duping spell over the entire world, who *knows* what they'd use the Seventh Stone for? These are the kind of people, Roxy, who order perfectly innocent fairies and gnomes – or whatever the heck Skinny is – to live in grotty out-of-the-way places, hidden away from the rest of the world. Make them get licences, like they're ... they're dogs, or something! Don't you think that's horrible? And don't you worry that if they can do it to them, they can do it to anyone else they turn against too?"

Roxy had to admit that Jones had a teeny-tiny point. OK, a massive point. It couldn't possibly be good for someone as power-hungry as Minister Splendid to get a hold of the most powerful magical object in the world, even if he wouldn't use it for Dark Magic himself.

"And just because MOOOOOH might not use it for Dark Magic," Jones went on, almost as if she'd read Roxy's mind, "that doesn't mean they'd be using it for anything *good*."

"All right!" Roxy held up both hands. "I actually agree. Maybe it would be better not to let the Ministry know we're on the trail. But you can't seriously be thinking of *carrying on* the trail, Jones, now you know how dangerous the Seventh Stone is! I mean, OK, when you were just looking for it to wreak revenge against your horrible stepmum, fine – and thanks for telling me the truth about that, by the way ..."

Jones gave a *pfffffft*, but at least had the decency to look slightly sheepish.

"... but now you know the Seventh Stone is the

kind of magical object that makes evil witches decide to break out of a top-security jail," Roxy went on, "do you *really* think we should carry on the hunt?"

"Sure, it's dangerous," Jones admitted. "But it sounds like things are going to get a lot *more* dangerous if that old witch finds the Stone before anyone else. You heard Frankie: nobody knows where it is. Well, you and I *almost* do. We have the best chance of stopping Bellissima getting her claws on it! In fact, if we *don't* try and find it now, we're pretty much letting the entire country down!"

Roxy knew when she was being manipulated. "Jones, we're just a couple of kids."

"Speak for yourself," retorted Jones, before going on in a deliberately look-how-sensible-I-can-be-when-I-put-my-mind-to-it voice. "Look, QG, I'll do you a deal. Once we've found the Stone, *then* we'll take it straight to some boring grown-up, OK? Though not to anyone at MOOOOOH, obviously."

"Maybe to Queen Ariadne?" Roxy was thinking out loud. "Or maybe to another minister, one that hates Minister Splendid so would never give it to him?"

"Exactly!"

"But then, Jones, why can't we just go and tell Queen Ariadne or one of those other ministers *right now*?"

"Because I'll just end up getting sent straight home, OK?" Jones suddenly snapped, throwing off the sensible voice as tetchily as she might have chucked off a serviceable-but-dull winter coat. "If we tell a grown-up, like a pair of boring old goody-goodies, they'll call my stepmother faster than you can say *cupcake incident*! I'll be back *there* again, in living misery! With memories of my dad everywhere, and my stepmother screaming at me, and my stepsisters making me tidy their rooms and clean their stinky loos, and…"

She stopped. She was breathing so heavily that her shoulders were rising and falling with the effort.

"Jones," Roxy said, reaching out to touch one of her shuddering shoulders. "I didn't realize it was that…"

Jones shot her such a fierce, wounded look that she didn't finish her sentence.

"OK," Roxy finished simply. "OK. We'll do it. We'll look for the Stone without telling anyone first."

Jones gave a curt nod of acknowledgement, then took one last, long deep breath, planted her usual devil-may-care grin back on her face and turned to open the door back to the storeroom. "So, Skinny," she said, striding through and giving him what she probably thought was a supportive thump on the arm, "Frankie was saying you knew some stuff about –" she

128

lowered her voice to a bare whisper – "witches?"

"Maybe I do." Skinny was red-eyed but he seemed to have recovered himself. "But like I said, this is a bad, bad time for anyone to be asking questions about them."

"Oh, but it's only one question. I'm looking for a witch's tower. Does that mean anything to you?"

Skinny blinked. "A *specific* witch's tower? Now, that could be tricky. A lot of witches used to live in towers in the olden days. It was kind of their thing." His gaze grew misty for a moment. "Ah, when I think back to some of the parties I went to in witches' towers—"

"Awesome," Jones interrupted. "But do you happen to know if any are still standing? Like, I'm sure a lot of witches' towers were knocked down in the Great Clean-Up, right?"

"Well, don't *badger* me, girl!" Skinny's misty gaze became a glare. "What is this, one of Wincey the Wisteria Fairy's interrogations or something?"

"Now, Skinny, dear, you really should call her by her official name," Frankie added nervously. "We must make sure we show the proper respect."

"RESPECT?" Skinny suddenly bellowed. "I've stepped in piles of dog poo I respect more than so-called Mrs Smith!"

"Oh, don't start all this again, dear…"

"I mean, I was a GOOD GUY!" yelled Skinny, now turning the colour of a ripe tomato. "But just because I accidentally *irked* her at the first Expedient Fiction Council meeting …"

"You called her a jumped-up lackey and a traitor to her people!" Frankie pointed out. "*And* told her she had rubbish taste in music!"

"… she made sure the Story Weavers wrote up my story TOTALLY WRONG!" Skinny finished. "And she *does* have rubbish taste in music. As it happens."

"Oooh," Jones said, "who are the Stor—"

"Do you have to know *absolutely blooming everything*?" Frankie interrupted Jones, before throwing up his hands in a cloud of lavender and exasperation. "The Story Weavers were the ones given the task of making the False Memory Enchantment watertight. They played around with troublesome bits of the kingdom's history and made sure that they'd be convincing as charming little stories instead."

"Charming little stories?" howled Skinny. "How'd *you* like it if you'd been turned into a villainous fairytale weirdo? I never did any of that bonkers baby-bartering stuff! All I ever did in that palace was quietly get on with managing the Weaving Department! Not to mention that it's total treachery of the so-called Smith woman to have ever taken on the job in the first place. She should never have agreed to work with that insufferable berk, Atticus Aren't-I-Terribly-Splendid, the way he's always despised us BOBIs, the way he's tried to erase us from the history of our own kingd—"

Skinny's rant was cut short by a sudden noise, so loud that it made them all jump. It was the sound of a large fist pounding, extremely hard, on the front door.

**13**

"OPEN UP!" yelled a voice to accompany the pounding fist. "SOUP MINISTRY OFFICIAL GUARD PATROL!"

Roxy, Jones, Frankie and Skinny stared at each other. Nobody dared move.

"OPEN UP!" yelled the voice again. "OR WE'LL BREAK THIS DOOR DOWN!"

This had Skinny unfrozen and out of his armchair faster than you could say *priceless old record collection*.

"That bunch of thugs!" he screeched, charging towards the shop.

"Skinny, no!" Frankie darted round to block his way. "You can't let them in!" he hissed. "You know I'm unlicensed!"

"WE KNOW AN UNLICENSED BOBI IS ON THE PREMISES," came the **SMOG**'s booming voice again. "I REPEAT, LET US IN OR WE WILL RUN AT THIS

DOOR WITH A BATTERING RAM."

"Well, that's just a waste of energy," said Jones. "Nobody needs a battering ram to break down a door as old and dodgy as that."

"How do they know you're here?" Roxy whispered. She reached for one of Frankie's hands, to soothe him as much as herself.

"The cameras all over Sector Seven, of course!" Skinny snapped. "They must have caught you nipping in here."

"The *what*?" squeaked Frankie.

"There are security cameras everywhere. Splendid's latest way to keep control of all us BOBIs. They'll be microchipping us next, like dogs, just you wait and see."

Frankie looked horrified. "And we'll be in even bigger trouble if they know we're harbouring two non-BOBIs!"

"WE KNOW YOU ARE HARBOURING TWO NON-BOBIs," came the **SMOG**'s voice again. "THIS IS IN DIRECT CONTRAVENTION OF EMERGENCY MAGIC-CONTROL ORDER NUMBER THREE-SIX-SIX, PARAGRAPH EIGHT, SUBSECTION TWENTY-NINE…"

The shouting, mercifully, stopped for a moment.

"CORRECTION," it came again, "I SHOULD

HAVE SAID PARAGRAPH TWENTY-NINE, SUB-
SECTION EIGHT. IT'S VERY NEW LEGISLATION.
I APOLOGIZE."

"What does Paragraph Twenty-Nine, Subsection
Eight actually *say*?" hissed Jones.

"ACCORDING TO THIS EMERGENCY LEGIS-
LATION," came the **SMOG**'s voice, "ANY BOBI
FOUND TO BE FRATERNIZING WITH A NON-
BOBI WITHOUT PRIOR PERMISSION, AND/OR
ENTERTAINING A NON-BOBI IN HIS/HER HOME,
WILL BE IMMEDIATELY ARRESTED, INVES-
TIGATED, CHARGED WITH TREASON AND SENT
TO JAIL. THE SAME APPLIES TO THE NON-BOBI."

*Treason? Jail?*

Roxy felt her head hit the floor.

She'd been knocked over by some sudden, invisible force... Hang on, what were those lilac-tinged
sparks still fizzing from Frankie's fingertips? And why
were the three of them – Frankie, Jones and Skinny
– all gazing at her with a mixture of horror and
astonishment?

"Did you just ... zap me?" she asked the fairy
godmother.

"I did." Frankie clapped a hand over his mouth.
"I was trying to make you invisible so you wouldn't get
discovered when the **SMOGs** come in."

"*Man*, am I glad you did Roxy first," said Jones, still open-mouthed.

"Don't worry, I'm OK," Roxy assured them, struggling to her feet. "No blood. No broken bones. No head injuries." She put a hand to her head to double-check this last assertion.

Well, that was odd.

Her hair didn't seem to stop in the right place, a few frizzy centimetres above her scalp.

It kept going.

And going.

And going.

It didn't *feel* like her normal hair, either. It was sticky and crystalline beneath her fingers, as if it had been covered with gallons of hairspray and lacquer.

"I think," said Frankie in a teeny-weeny voice, "that instead of an Instant Invisibility Spell, I might eeeeeeever-so-slightly-accidentally have done another of my Miracle Makeover charms."

"How bad is it?" Roxy managed to croak.

"It's bad," said Jones. "It's a metre-high apricot-blonde up-do."

"It's not *bad*," snapped Frankie.

"You're right," said Jones. "It's *awful*—"

She was interrupted by the same clear, crisp voice

they'd heard in the Septagon earlier. Mrs Smith had evidently taken control of the megaphone.

"I know you're in there, Francesca the Flotsam Fairy," she called pleasantly.

Frankie reddened at the use of his full name and the others turned to stare at him.

"Won't you let us in, Francesca," Mrs Smith went on, "so we can sit down and talk about all of this? Nobody wants any trouble. Least of all those innocent girls we know you're sheltering."

"Back door!" said Skinny, pointing at the tatty striped curtains. "Behind there. Go!"

"I'm not leaving you, Skinny!" Frankie shrieked.

"Not *you*! You're staying here with me to sort this mess out. I meant *them*!" Skinny jerked a thumb at Jones and Roxy.

"Hey!" Jones put her hands on her hips. "We can totally look after ourselves! A bunch of bully-boys like that doesn't scare me!"

"Um, it scares me a bit," Roxy mumbled. "Look, you don't understand," she went on as Jones glared at her. "I can't have my sister getting into trouble because of me. She needs that cleaning job! It's all we have. I'm not being a cowardly custard, or whatever you were thinking, it's just—"

"Fine!" Jones snapped, already striding to the

curtains and pulling them back. "But this is NOT running away. This is a *tactical retreat*."

"Good," said Skinny. "Now, you'll need to take Seven Point Three Street all the way to the end, then head into the junkyard. Go through the gap in the fence at the end and you'll be out on the open road again. Don't go any other way. They'll have put up roadblocks."

"They have!" gasped Frankie. "They said so!"

"You'll be fine once you're out of the Sector. But be quick about it. I'll stall them for a minute." Skinny gave the girls a brief salute, eyes gleaming. "Oh, and that witch stuff you were talking about? You'll be wanting to speak to Mortadella. If there's a witch's tower still standing in Illustria, she'll know about it."

"Mortadella?" Roxy recognized the name. "You don't mean ... the evil fairy who cursed Sleeping Beauty?"

"Evil fairies *are* witches," said Skinny. "Or near enough. And don't let the whole cursing thing put you off. Mortadella's changed. A *lot*. Runs a kind of spiritual retreat these days, for stressed-out witches."

"Oooh, yes, I've heard it's amazing," said Frankie longingly. "More like a fabulous spa hotel, really. And Skinny's right, now I think of it: Mortadella should be able to tell you anything you want to know."

There was an ear-splitting, wood-splintering crash

137

at the front of the shop. It sounded a lot like the batter-ing ram was being put to use.

"All right, all right!" yelled Skinny. "Give a bloke a moment to find his keys, won't you?"

The striped curtains, now pulled back, had revealed the grimiest French windows Roxy had ever seen; the handle worked, though, and Jones slid the door open and stepped through.

"Come on," she said, reaching back for Roxy's hand. Roxy crouched as low as she could, and the enormous pile of stiff hair made it through. "So now what?" Jones finished, glancing up the road as Frankie followed them out. "We *run*? How's that going to work, then, with old Big Hair here?"

"Frankie," begged Roxy, clutching her hair. "*Please* can you un-magic it?"

"No can do, dear, sorry." Frankie was rooting in his handbag. "Don't worry, most of my spells are pre-set to end at the stroke of midnight. And talking of magic…" He pulled out the shiny aubergine he'd shown them earlier. "Cross your fingers, girls!"

"Frankie, no!" Roxy grabbed for the aubergine, but it was too late. Frankie had already tossed it into the air. A shower of now-rather-familiar lilac sparks flew from his fingers, and—

"Step back, dearies!" Frankie shrieked, only a split

second before a large and extremely shiny purple motorbike slammed down onto the cobblestones right in front of the girls.

In the silence that followed, they could hear Skinny's voice again, back inside the store.

"Now, there's no need for any stress, Wincey, old girl," he was saying, "I know those keys are around somewhere. You've just got to give me a mo…"

"Frankie." Jones was gazing at the bike with an expression Roxy hadn't seen on her before. It looked a lot like *love*. "Have you seriously just magicked up a vehicle from a vegetable?"

"Do you know, dear, I rather think I have!"

"Then you are officially the most awesome fairy godmother *ever*!" Jones let out a whoop and swung her leg over the motorbike. "Oh, wow," she breathed, popping the lilac fedora back on her head. It looked rather like the hat had become hers.

"Girls, really, you need to go now. As soon as you're safely out of Sector Seven, you need to head to the Fabulous Forest, OK? You'll find Mortadella's retreat there."

"Fabulous Forest?" Roxy couldn't hide her surprise. "I've been there once, on a school trip. It's just full of artificial rapids for white-water rafting, and campsites and stuff."

"That's only the outskirts. When you reach the Forest, keep driving northwards – keep on driving, *no matter how thick the forest gets* – and you'll eventually reach the dead centre. That's where Mortadella's retreat is hidden. Now go!"

Roxy, on shaking legs, clambered onto the back of the motorbike behind Jones. It felt firm and reassuringly metallic, and it gave off only the faintest vegetal whiff.

"Frankie," she croaked, "will you be OK?"

"Don't you worry about me, dearie! And don't *you* worry about me either," he added, rather pointedly, at Jones, who was completely taken with her new toy and already revving the engine impatiently. "Skinny and I will think of something to get the **SMOGs** off our backs. Will you two just promise me – whatever the reason you want to find this witch's tower – you're not doing anything *too* dangerous?"

Roxy opened her mouth to reply.

But perhaps it was a good thing that, at that moment, Jones pressed hard on the handlebars and, with a shout of thanks in Frankie's direction, sped the aubergine motorbike along Seven Point Three Street, towards the Fabulous Forest.

## 14

Thanks to a killer combo of the sat-nav on Roxy's phone plus the remarkable speed of what Jones was already calling the Veg-E-Bike, they were already deep into the Fabulous Forest only a couple of hours after speeding away from Sector Seven.

"My sat-nav's getting a bit confused," Roxy yelled over the noise of the engine. "Must be all the trees. But remember what Frankie said: we just keep heading north, no matter how thick the forest gets."

"No prob!" Jones yelled back. "Anyway, I'm glad it's getting a bit wilder, after all those creepily perfect campsites and that piddly little so-called lake! Rubbish school trip you must have had, staying there! Not like this proper adventure!"

Roxy wanted to agree – to be fair, nothing could have been worse than the four days she'd spent at

Camp Good-Times with sixty-two of her old class-mates – but she couldn't shake off the anxious ache in the pit of her stomach. Actually, she couldn't shake off *anything*, not with this appalling heap of hair weighing her down.

"Just to be clear, there's *nothing* I can do about the hair," Roxy yelled, "until the magic wears off at midnight?"

"Nope! I mean, I guess you could try and let it down. But then we'll just have about ten miles of tresses trailing behind us!" Jones yelled back. "If you're worrying about what your sister will say, don't – it'll all be back to normal by the next time she sees you!"

This had been precisely what Roxy had been worrying about but hadn't wanted to say.

"Um, on that front, Jones," she began, tightening her hold round Jones's waist with the arm that wasn't being used to steady her hair. "We won't stay too long at this witch spa-retreat place, right? I mean, we have to be back in Rexopolis by bedtime, obviously."

Jones snorted. "Yeah, right. Because *that's* what people do when they're trying to *save their entire country from an evil witch*: pop back home at the end of the day for their jim-jams and slippers."

"But I *have* to go back home tonight." Unease was spreading through Roxy's gut; had she bitten off more than she could chew? "You don't understand. My sister, she gets … anxious."

"Maybe you shouldn't join me at all, then. I mean, if your sister's going to get *anxious*. Maybe you should leave before we even meet Mortadella, and head home, and spend the rest of the day doing … sorry, what *exactly* were you doing when I met you this morning? Sitting on your own listening to music, with breakfast cereal stuck to your face?"

"OK, OK." Roxy could feel her cheeks heating up. "I get it."

"*Do* you, Roxy? Because you can't be here if you're not properly up for it. This is BIG STUFF. We're saving the world!"

"I thought you just said we were saving our *country*," Roxy muttered mutinously.

"Yeah, but you heard Frankie and Skinny. The Perpetual Wickedness – sorry, sorry, I mean Pep-Wick! – could return and infest Illustria again. And if Dark Magic can infest Illustria, it's only a matter of time before it infests the entire planet! And the only thing standing between old Bellissima and an all-powerful Witching Stone is us. You and me, kid!"

Roxy couldn't pretend that a shiver of excitement hadn't just whizzed its way up her spine. Especially not when – *how?* – Jones seemed to have noticed it too.

"I felt that!" Jones cackled as she steered the Veg-E-Bike impressively between two densely wooded evergreens. The track was getting narrower and the daylight more sparse with every quarter of a mile. "You've got a bit of hero lurking in you somewhere after all! OK, a pretty well-hidden bit of hero, but still…"

"Hey. Just because I don't go around *deliberately* seeking out danger!" Roxy protested. Then she fell silent for a moment. She was busy thinking. Or rather, for the first time in her life perhaps, *not* thinking. "Look, I don't want evil Queen Bellissima to find this Seventh Witching Stone any more than you do …"

"Fighting talk!" Jones punched the air, then quickly returned her hand to the handlebars before they swerved off course.

"… and after hearing what happened to poor Skinny's sister… If anything like that ever happened to my sister…" Roxy was feeling a bit sick again, and the bumpity-bump of the Veg-E-Bike on the forest track wasn't helping. "But maybe you'd be better off on your own. I just don't know if I'm cut out for all this stuff."

"Well, nobody ever *knows* if they're cut out for this stuff. Not until they at least *try*. And Fate has chosen us, kid. No – *Destiny*! Destiny has thrown you and me together, you with your crazy super-memory and me with all my incredibly awesome skills that would take way too long to list – and by the way, one of my most awesome skills is my modesty." Jones paused because the Veg-E-Bike had just let out the most colossal farting noise. "I mean, has it ever occurred to you," she went on, "that maybe you were given that gift of yours *for a reason*?"

This had, obviously, never occurred to Roxy for even a single minute.

"Because the way I see it, *everything* happens for a reason," Jones was musing. "Like, all that time I was treated like dirt by my stepfamily. Yeah, it was horrible, being made to sleep in the attic with no heating and not even a proper bed, for Pete's sake …"

"Jones, look, if you ever need to talk about all that—"

"… but all that stuff taught me something," Jones interrupted. "It taught me how important it is to be *free*. And I'll tell you one thing: now that I know what my own hard-won freedom feels like, there's *no way on earth* I'm letting some Dark Magic tyrant come and stamp all over it. Or letting it happen to anyone else, for that matter. And freedom, by the way, doesn't just *turn up*. It doesn't pop round for a nice cup of tea when you least expect it. Freedom is something you have to get out there and fight for. It's something you have to win. You can't rely on anyone else to do that for you. And if I – if *we* – can be the ones who make sure our country is never again enslaved by Dark Magic ... well, that'll make us heroes, kid. Proper, epic *heroes*."

At which point in this incredibly stirring speech, the Veg-E-Bike farted again and then stopped altogether.

And then, just as suddenly, it turned back into an aubergine, tumbling the two of them onto the forest floor.

"Nice time for *that* to happen!" howled Jones, kicking the aubergine in frustration, then hitting it with Frankie's fedora for good measure. "So much for Frankie's spells lasting until the stroke of midnight! It's not even the stroke of half past blooming three!"

"And *now* how are we going to get back home by nightfall?" Roxy staggered to her feet, still clutching her atrocious hair. "Let alone find this witches' retreat place!"

"Well, we'll just have to keep going." Jones picked up her fallen kitbag, popped the fedora back on and began to stride on up the track. "D'you know," she added, craning her neck to peer up at the overhanging tree branches, heavy above them, "I can't help wondering if this so-called Fabulous Forest might have been *another* forest in the days of the Cursed Kingdom. Like, maybe, the forest that sprang up around Sleeping Beauty's castle while she slept for a hundred years."

"You think so, do you?" sighed Roxy, trudging after her. (She might have been more able to throw herself square behind some of Jones's crazy plans to Save the World, she decided, if she didn't feel quite so tired, hungry and footsore.)

"Well, have you ever seen a forest quite this thick?" Jones was using her hands to shove aside a particularly thorny hedge that the Veg-E-Bike would never have got through anyway. "I'll bet Minister Splendid's guys gave up cutting it back when it all got too wild. They probably thought nobody would ever come as deep as this, anywaaaaaaaaayyyy..."

The last word faded into an awed sigh as, on the other side of the thorny briar, a truly magnificent sight greeted their eyes.

Through the briar was a clearing, and in the middle of the clearing stood a palace. It was built from palest yellow stone, and its half-dozen dreamy turrets were circled with rambling pink roses. The palace was surrounded by lush green lawns and a sweeping gravelled drive with marble fountains, an ornamental pond and sculpted hedges. One looked a lot like a cauldron, another like a broomstick...

"It's the witches' retreat!" gasped Roxy, pointing at the sign positioned between two hedges:

## WELCOME TO MORTADELLA'S WOEBEGONE-WITCH WELLNESS CENTRE AND MAGICAL RETREAT

In swirling gold letters beneath this was written what looked like a motto: *COME UNTO US AND REST YOUR WEARY CAULDRONS*.

"This is so awesome!" breathed Jones.

*Awesome* wasn't exactly how Roxy would have described it, especially now that a golf cart was trundling towards them. Her knees were knocking together in fear. The person climbing out of the golf cart, though, looked absolutely nothing like a witch. She was wearing black, it was true, but leggings and a cosy hoodie rather than a witchy robe, and her skin was glowing and lightly tanned. There was not a wart or a hooked nose in sight.

"Welcome," she said, in a mellifluous chime. She joined her hands together in a yoga pose and bowed briefly. "I am Katalina, Guest Services Team. Welcome to Mortadella's Woebegone-Witch Wellness Centre and Magical Retreat. Come unto us and rest your weary cauldrons."

"Actually," Roxy squeaked, "we're not—"

Jones kicked her, hard, on the ankle.

"Yeah, we are pretty woebegone," Jones said. "I mean, it's tough being a young witch these days. So much to worry about: is my broomstick fast enough, is my bat, er, batty enough?"

Katalina nodded kindly. "It's the sort of thing we hear a lot here at Mortadella's. Let me take you up to Reception," she went on, climbing back into the golf cart and motioning for them to join her, "and we can get you witchlets all checked in."

"Awesome! Though I should just say, we haven't necessarily decided to *stay* yet," Jones said, pulling Roxy into the cart beside her (thanks to the hair, Roxy had to lean sideways at an extremely uncomfortable angle). "We'd like to ask a few important questions first."

"Certainly. Many of our witches have questions." Katalina started the golf cart, which began to glide so smoothly across the gravel that Roxy couldn't help wondering if it wasn't in fact gliding *on* the gravel at all, but slightly *above* it. *"Who am I? What is the meaning of life? Can I really express my magical self in a harsh world that no longer cares?"*

"Excellent questions, all." Jones stuck up a thumb as the golf cart stopped beside the steps that led up to the palace's magnificent glass front door. "And, y'know, *is there a witch's tower still standing anywhere in the country, and if so, where is it?*"

Katalina's eyebrows rose up her smooth forehead. "I don't think I've ever heard that one before. But here's our wonderful director. I'm sure Mortadella will be able to help you with anything you need."

Roxy, who now had a really nasty crick in her neck, looked up awkwardly to see a figure descending the marble steps.

So this was Mortadella.

## 15

If Katalina was serene, Mortadella was positively ethereal: even less like a witch, more of an angel. Her black hair was cropped close to her heart-shaped face, and her huge green eyes shone warmly at the new arrivals. She was wearing a white version of Katalina's leggings-and-hoodie combo, with the words **HEX. SLEEP. MEDITATE. REPEAT** printed in gold lettering on the front.

"Good afternoon, witchlets," she began in a voice like a warm bed, "and welcome to—"

She was interrupted by the loudest BANG-CRASH Roxy had ever heard.

Roxy shrieked. Even Jones gave a small squeak.

"Oh, don't worry about that!" Mortadella beamed, beatifically. "That's just our witch transport landing. Kat, my love, go and tell the driver to take it out of

Invisibility Mode so these witchlets can see it."

Katalina strolled about ten metres and leaned forwards slightly, and her entire top half disappeared.

"We have to give our witch transport an Invisibility Shield," Mortadella explained as Roxy and Jones's mouths fell open, "to deliver our guests safely from all over the country. Can you imagine the *trouble* from MOOOOOH if any witches were spotted in the skies on their broomsticks? Fines, shutdowns... You two didn't come by broomstick, did you?"

"No, no." Jones, unlike Roxy, had recovered enough to speak. "We ... uh ... walked."

"Well, I hope you *packed* your broomsticks nevertheless. We have some fabulous broomstick-yoga classes here at the retreat! Ah, Invisibility Shield well and truly off!"

Where there had, a moment ago, merely been a half-Katalina, there was suddenly an *entire* Katalina, leaning into a gleaming white minibus. **MORTADELLA'S WOEBEGONE-WITCH WELLNESS CENTRE AND MAGICAL RETREAT** was written on the outside in silvery lettering, and through the tinted windows the girls could just see a few weary figures getting up out of their seats. As they watched, Katalina began to help them off the minibus: defeated-looking women ranging from fairly young to rather old, carrying overnight cases, yoga mats and broomsticks.

"More woebegone witches in need of our care," Mortadella said gravely before turning and swanning back up the steps. "Let's get you two witchlets checked in before the rush."

"Jones, we can't do this!" Roxy hissed. "Carry on pretending we're witches, I mean. And we definitely cannot *stay* here!"

"Relax," Jones hissed back. "We'll just find out what we need to know and then get the *hex* out of here." She chuckled at her own joke before bounding up the steps to join Mortadella. Roxy staggered up after her, struggling under the weight of her hair, and reached them just as the glass door opened.

"Wow," breathed Jones. "This is *epic*."

They were in a kind of atrium, but one with no ceiling: just open sky way above their heads. More marble fountains divided the vast hall into smaller sections: a chill-out zone with squashy white bean bags and cauldron-shaped mugs stacked up beside a tea urn; an area with brightly coloured exercise mats where a group of women of various shapes and sizes did indeed seem to be doing some kind of yoga on their broomsticks; a little snack stall and some tables dotted among palm fronds where witch guests in white towelling robes sat with pots of tea and plates of cake.

"Goji-berry-and-bran muffins today," Mortadella said with a smile as she saw Jones's nose twitch. "One hundred per cent vegan, and *so* good for you!"

"Oh." Jones looked disappointed.

"I'm very proud of this whole place," Mortadella added, gazing around with Roxy and Jones as if seeing it through their eyes. "Let's face it, we witches have always needed a safe place. Never more so than these past twenty years."

"For sure," agreed Jones. "So, look, before we check in, I have this weirdly specific question—"

"And I have a few questions for you, too," Mortadella interrupted, opening the door to an office just off the atrium. This was another beautiful, rather sparse room, with huge windows and wooden floors. An elegant vase of lilies stood on a glass coffee table at the centre of a small circle of white leather bean bag chairs. She sank elegantly into one of these chairs. "Well, just *one* question, actually," she went on regarding them with her deep green eyes. "Why are you lying about being witches?"

Roxy's hands tightened on her hair-do. Beside her she could feel Jones stiffen too.

"Who says we're not witches?" Jones mumbled.

"Oh, darlings!" Mortadella laughed quite kindly. "Even if I hadn't known the moment I saw you, I'm afraid you gave yourselves away when you couldn't see past the Invisibility Shield on the enchanted minibus! But don't worry, girls. I'm not here to judge you. There is *no judgement* at the retreat." She raised a theatrical hand to one side of her face to whisper, "Well, perhaps only if you're really, really bad at broomstick yoga."

Neither of them laughed.

"Look, we're not here to do anything bad!" Jones blurted out. "We just need to talk to a witch. We need a bit of witch-based information."

"*Information?*" Mortadella's serene gaze clouded slightly. Jones's answer had evidently taken her by surprise. Perhaps, Roxy wondered, she had thought they'd snuck in for her autograph or something. "May I ask, please, precisely who you are working for?"

"Oh, no, we're not working for anyone. Just ourselves. I'm a treasure hunter, see – well, a *collector*, maybe I should say – of ancient artefacts, and..."

"So you aren't agents of Minister Splendid?"

"Too blooming right we're not!" snorted Jones.

"We know what he's done to your people," Roxy added hastily. "We certainly wouldn't work for a man like him."

"Oh, the Minister isn't so bad really. I frequently work with his agents – I help them out with information they need; they leave us alone – it's a good arrangement. After all, we're both on the same side against Dark Magic." Mortadella was watching them very closely now. "My question to you girls is: *are you?*"

"Are we what?" Roxy asked stupidly, and then stopped. There was, quite suddenly, a pulling sensation in her forehead, right between her eyes. It was gentle and not-at-all unpleasant, rather like having a head massage from the inside, and it was clear that Jones must be feeling a similar sensation, because she was rubbing her forehead with the heel of her hand and frowning as if wondering what was going on in there.

"Are you on the side of Diabolica?" Mortadella asked softly. The pulling sensation increased for a moment and then stopped, just as suddenly as it had started. "I can see," the witch announced, her face relaxing into its serene beam again, "that you are not. I am reassured that your hearts are pure. Well, *mostly* pure," she added with an elegant wink in Jones's direction. "Might I advise, for your own sake, that you let go of your burning anger towards your stepfamily? Harbouring a desire for vengeance will destroy you more than it will destroy them."

"Hey!" Jones looked astonished. "How on earth did you…?"

"Now you, my dear child…" Mortadella was

peering at Roxy, far more intently than she had looked at Jones, and with an expression of rapt fascination. "*You* are more of a mystery to me, though I cannot tell why."

Roxy couldn't help feeling a tiny bit chuffed for a moment. She'd never been mysterious before, not once in her whole entire life.

"*She's* the mysterious one?" Jones sounded faintly put out. "What's *she* got to be so mysterious about?"

"Plenty!" Mortadella was still gazing at Roxy. "Of course, there's the obvious secret right at the surface: the secret that she keeps about her half-brother, the world-famous rock star. But I'm struggling to go any deeper—"

"What on earth do you mean," Jones interrupted, "*her half-brother, the world-famous rock star*? She doesn't *have* a half-brother who's a world-famous rock star."

"Um," muttered Roxy. "I kind of do, actually."

"WHO?"

Roxy took a slow, deep breath. "H-Bomb."

"*H-Bomb is your brother?*" gasped Jones.

"Yes."

"From H-Bomb and the Missiles?"

"Yes."

"But he's … incredible."

"Yes."

157

"And you're so … average."

"Thanks."

"Sorry, I don't mean that." Jones looked abashed. "You're normal, that's what I meant."

"Compared to my super-talented, world-famous, rock-star half-brother? Yes. I am."

"Oh, this is good," urged Mortadella, leaning in and raising her hands in a praying gesture. "This is *healing*."

This was all just getting plain *weird*, Roxy thought, and what had happened to Jones's single-minded desire to dig out the information about the witch's tower and then *get the hex out of here*?

"Hang on," Jones said. She frowned. "His real name is Hansel, right?"

"Yes. Hansel Humperdinck. We call him Han, mostly."

"Huh. That's so weird. Your brother and sister are called Hansel and Gretel."

"Oh." Roxy blinked. "That's … that's true."

"Well, I'm sure it's just a coincidence. I mean, the chances that your brother and sister were actually *the* Hansel and Gretel, the same ones that got captured by a child-eating witch and held prisoner in a gingerbread house, the ones with the horrible stepmother and the cowardly dad…" Jones stopped. Her forehead creased. "You said your dad has had other wives, didn't you?"

"Yes." Roxy had started to feel sick. "And … my brother and sister had one stepmother who was so horrible they never even talk about her."

"Riiiiiight. Still, it's unlikely that it really *was* them. I expect they'd still be freaked out by it all, even now they're grown up. Like, phobic about sweets or something."

There was a pause. "My sister *is* phobic about sweets."

"Ah," said Jones. "Yeah. You mentioned that. But hold on! Hansel and Gretel took all the witch's treasure when they escaped, right? So they'd be incredibly rich."

"My *dad* is incredibly rich," whispered Roxy. "He's never said where he got his money from, but my brother and sister have never wanted a penny of it. No matter how little they've had themselves. His money always made them sick."

There was a brief silence.

"OK, so this is major-league awks," said Jones, shifting on her feet and fiddling with her hat. "I'm … uh … I'm not all that good with, y'know, emotions and all that stuff…"

"You were about to tell me," Mortadella interrupted

159

graciously, "about this witch-based information you are seeking?"

Roxy was grateful to Mortadella for the smooth change of subject, but she could hardly stop her own mind tumbling.

"And something else…" she mumbled. "My brother's songs … most of them are about witches."

"Oh, I wouldn't say *most*… I mean, yes, there is that one about the pale green skin and the warts on the nose. And true, there's 'Here I Am, Stuck in the Cauldron With You'. Oooh, and there's the one where he sings about being locked in a cage…" Jones stopped when she saw Roxy's face. "So," she said quickly to Mortadella, "we're on this kind of mission, you see. I don't know if you've heard anything about a certain E-V-I-L S-P-I-R-I-T escaping from a certain M-O-U-N-T-A-I-N P-R-I-S-O-N?"

"Ah," Mortadella sighed. "We have all heard the rumours, yes. It's why I thought you might be Minister Splendid's agents. Whenever there's imminent magical danger they want our help, and believe me, there's no bigger danger than this."

"Which is why we're on the case!" said Jones proudly. "We're looking for something that's been described as *a witch's tower*. Do you have any idea where that might be?"

"Well, that would almost certainly be my dear friend Witchalina McWitch's family fortress! The McWitches are the only family whose tower is still standing. MOOOOOH tore down most of them during the Great Clean-Up, but they allowed the McWitch family to remain in their home in return for keeping an eye on the mountains. After all, the tower is right at the foot of the Blizzy Lizzy Mountains. If any Diabolicals escaped prison, they would have to pass them."

"Perfect," Jones breathed. "So it can't be too far from here, right? The mountains are only a hundred miles from Rexopolis, and we've driven fifty miles of that already."

"Not far at all. Let me look up the exact address so you can pop it into your sat-nav." Mortadella reached into the pocket of her hoodie and pulled out a phone in a rather snazzy diamanté phone case. She scrolled for a moment. *"Witchalina McWitch, Witch End, North Road, BL2 1WW."* She turned her phone so the girls could read it from the screen.

"Got that?" Jones asked Roxy.

Roxy blinked at the screen, still dazed. "Yes. But I don't want to go up there with you, Jones. I just want to go home."

"Come on, QG!"

"I mean it. I want… No, I *need* to go home. I'm

161

sorry. Oh," Roxy muttered as a text message popped up on Mortadella's phone, looking – oddly – as if it had been written in Latin. "There's a message for you."

Mortadella took back the phone. "Oh, that's wonderful news! My spell provider has just updated an outmoded enchantment."

"Awesome," said Jones abruptly. She was staring at Roxy. "Kid, you can't actually *do* this. You're letting me down. You're letting yourself down!"

"I'm going home, Jones." Roxy couldn't meet her friend's eye. "You can't persuade me otherwise."

"Great." Jones's voice was heavy with bitterness. "Well, then. So, I guess, if you're not cut out for saving the world, there's nothing I can—"

"Perhaps," interrupted Mortadella brightly, taking Jones's arm, "you'd like to come with me to our fabulous Spell-ness Zone, and see my lovely new spell put into action? Give your friend a moment by herself to clear her head?"

For once, Jones seemed to recognize a pointed tone when she heard one.

"Yeah, all right." She stood up and followed Mortadella to the office door. "Look, I can't *make* you stick this out," she said, turning back to Roxy for a moment. "But all I can say is this: now we've come this far, I'll be blooming unimpressed if you bottle it."

## 16

As the door closed behind Jones and Mortadella, Roxy walked out of the atrium and down the marble steps outside.

She hadn't the faintest clue yet if she was leaving Jones behind for good or just needed to clear her head.

Roxy sat down rather suddenly on the bottom step.

It was fair to say that, of all the astonishing things that had happened to her so far today, this one was the biggest shock of all.

She'd read the story of Hansel and Gretel just once, in a tattered *Child's Treasury of Fairytales* borrowed from the library, and she knew it – obviously – word for word.

Now she closed her eyes and summoned up the book's pages in her mind's eye.

Once upon a time, in a dark, dark wood, lived a

brother and sister named Hansel and Gretel...

OK, so where *was* this dark, dark wood? According to Gretel – who dodged any questions Roxy had ever asked about their lives before she was born – she and Han had grown up in "south-east Illustria", near Awesomeland theme park and the border with Placedonia.

They lived with their father and their stepmother, a cruel and heartless woman who wished to be rid of them...

Roxy raked over the fragments of what she knew about the stepmothers her brother and sister had had before she was born. They'd definitely mentioned one called Babs, a foul-sounding woman with the habit of cancelling birthdays. Then there was Marcie, who'd done something unspeakable to Gretel's pet kitten. Really, it was hard to think of any stepmother they'd had who *hadn't* come under the category of Cruel and Heartless ... not to mention That One they never spoke about.

Roxy was thinking so hard about Gretel, and the little she'd told her about their early lives, that it was not, at first, a terrible shock to see Gretel herself walking across the gravel drive towards her. In fact, she almost thought she must be imagining it.

But no. It. Really. Was. Gretel.

For a moment – a long, *horrible* moment – Roxy assumed Gretel had come for her.

Yet right now, it didn't even look like Gretel had seen her. She was too busy talking into her phone.

"… sure, I can do that," Gretel was saying. "I'll need a dozen of our best guys, though."

Roxy scrambled off the steps. Crouching low, she ran as fast as she could towards the only object large enough to shield her from view: the minibus.

"… obviously we're all focussed on the prison break right now," Gretel was saying. "Yes, Minister Splendid… No, Minister Splendid… I do appreciate that you're upset your daughter's head has been turned into a tropical fruit, sir, but I don't think that could possibly have anything to do with Bellissima…"

Gretel's voice sounded *weird*.

Still bossy, yes, but with none of the usual peevish weariness. This was a completely different kind of bossy: clipped and dynamic and no-nonsense. And why on earth was she talking to *Minister Splendid* about the *prison break*? Surely, if she ever spoke to her boss at all, it would be about his loo?

Not to mention the fact that none of this sounded AT ALL like Gretel was here to track down her rule-breaking little sister.

Roxy, her back flat against the minibus, used the

wing mirror to spy on Gretel, who had now reached the palace steps.

She wasn't wearing her pebbly glasses. Her mousy hair was pulled into a sleek, high ponytail. Her grey loo-cleaner overalls had been replaced by an ankle-length scarlet Puffa coat, and on her feet were – *no!* – high-heeled lipstick-red boots.

Gretel didn't wear high heels. Certainly not bright red ones. Gretel wore fluffy slippers the colour of cowpats, and cleaner's rubber clogs the colour of, well, cowpats.

"I'll ask Mrs Smith when I see her, sir," she was saying. "She's heading straight here from Sector Seven... Well, I should think she'll be here any minute now, sir... No, sir, there's no suspicion any of Mortadella's witches are involved in the breakout," she added, more sharply than before. "None at all. We're just here for her help."

Baffling though all this was – especially given the fact that Gretel had claimed nobody called Mrs Smith even existed – Roxy tried to focus on the important information. Which was that Mrs Smith was going to be here, at the retreat, *any minute now*.

And Jones was still inside.

If anything was going to put paid to Jones's mission to save the country – nay, the entire world – it was

166

Mrs Smith and her **SMOG** units catching them. And charging them with treason. And locking them up without a trial.

Roxy had to do something, fast.

Gretel was still standing on the front steps. There was no way Roxy could get past her without being recognized. No, not even with Frankie's appalling hair-do: it was ghastly, but it hardly qualified as a disguise.

"I'm quite sure the fruit-head thing will wear off soon, sir." Gretel was wandering away from the entrance now as she continued to talk on the phone. "Yes, I will ask Mrs Smith if she knows a counter-spell, but I don't want to put her in a bad mood about unauthorized magic, sir. You know I've already got my doubts about her recent methods…"

Roxy, unnerved by how close Gretel was getting, scurried into the minibus. She crouched on the floor for a moment, beside the driver's seat, and looked around.

Immediately beside the tip of her right ear was a control panel, just like those on a normal car or bus, with a key to start the ignition, a button for the wind-screen wipers and a button to turn up the heating. But Roxy could see several buttons unlike any she'd seen in a vehicle before.

One said **INVISIBILITY SHIELD** and the other said **FLIGHT MODE**.

Not stopping to think – this was not the time to *think*, even for a split second – Roxy reached up a hand and turned the ignition key. Then she slammed down on the **INVISIBILITY SHIELD** button.

"Of course, sir, I have the utmost respect for Mrs— Oh!" Gretel sounded surprised – as well she might do, seeing as the large white minibus that had been parked only a few metres away had suddenly disappeared. "No, nothing to worry about, sir. A minor hex incident. I ought to be used to them by now… No, of course I'm not suggesting your daughter should just get used to having a fruit for a face for the rest of her life, sir…"

Roxy glanced down at her hands, reassured that, however invisible she might be from the outside, she was at least still visible to herself. Peeping up to get a better view through the windscreen, she saw that Gretel had turned again and was heading back towards the palace's entrance.

Then, heart hammering, she hit the button that said **FLIGHT MODE**.

It felt like her stomach had remained on the ground while the rest of her shot straight up into the air. She grabbed the back of the driver's seat just to have something to hang on to, and then dragged herself into it so that she could take the steering wheel. She felt as if she were still shooting upwards, and this was confirmed by a dial on the dashboard, divided into four sections: **HIGH; HIGHER; WOW, YOU'RE HIGH NOW** and **DESTINATION MARS???** The needle was shooting past **HIGHER** and just into **WOW, YOU'RE HIGH NOW** when she saw a **CRUISE CONTROL** button to the left of the **FLIGHT MODE** one. Desperately, she pressed it. The bus stopped shooting upwards and hovered, almost uncertainly, for a second, before Roxy decided to just go for it and press her foot down on the accelerator.

Pleasingly smoothly, the minibus glided forwards.

Roxy knew she had to steer, and not just because if she didn't she would crash smack-wallop into one of the rose-covered palace turrets. This was a less smooth endeavour – the bus jerked frighteningly to the left as she over-steered, then lurched horrifyingly to the right as she over-corrected. But somehow she had managed to sail between two of the turrets without catastrophe.

"Result!" She grinned, feeling more like Jones, in this moment, than she had ever thought possible.

But she was only at the beginning of her rescue mission. Through the windscreen, she had a bird's-eye view of the open-air atrium, and it was not hard to spot Mortadella and Jones: the white-clad figure beside the small one in the lilac hat standing – of *course* – beside what she recognized as the little snack stall.

Taking a deep breath, Roxy reached for the final button on the control panel, the one that said **SMOOTH LANDING**.

And smooth it really was. The invisible minibus didn't plummet downwards anywhere near as fast as it had shot upwards, but instead sank back towards the ground in an almost stately fashion. It even gave Roxy time to steer it in precisely the direction of the snack stall.

Then two things happened at once. First, Roxy saw Gretel, in her snappy red coat, appear from the right side of the atrium, making a beeline towards Mortadella and Jones. Second, Roxy realized she did not in fact want to make a **SMOOTH LANDING**, or indeed a **LANDING** of any kind at all.

This was going to require some *serious* cool-under-pressure.

Thankfully, the doors of the minibus were still open, and juuuuuust close enough for Roxy to lean out without having to get entirely out of the driver's seat.

"… so if you don't mind, before you show me this amazing new spell of yours," Jones was saying to Mortadella, "I'd quite like to try one of these goji-berry-and-bran muffins you mentioned earlier. I mean, I'm not much of a bran fan, to be honest with you, but I'm absolutely blooming starving, and..."

"Mortadella," said Gretel as she reached them. "Good to see you again. Can we talk in—"

Simultaneously, Roxy reached one hand through the minibus doors and pressed the **FLIGHT MODE** button with the other.

She just had time, before the bus shot up into the air again, to see Gretel's astonished face as a hand appeared, seemingly from nowhere, and hoicked the small, midnight-blue-haired girl up into ... where? As far as Gretel was concerned, this girl had disappeared into thin air leaving behind nothing but the brown boot that had fallen off her foot.

"Mortadella," Gretel began, "what the blithering *heck* is going on around here?"

"Ah, dear Ms Humperdinck!" Mortadella was giving a little yoga bow of greeting, hands together. "What a pleasant surprise!"

"Hey, don't pretend that didn't just happen!"

"What didn't just happen?" Mortadella sounded as innocent as a newborn. "Now," she went on, deftly and deliberately steering Gretel away from the scene of Jones's mysterious disappearance, "can I interest you in a delicious soy-milk smoothie?"

But as the minibus was already ten, fifteen, twenty metres in the air again, Roxy couldn't hear her sister's reply.

Jones, sprawled on the minibus floor, stared in exactly the same kind of astonishment as Roxy pressed the **CRUISE CONTROL** button and began to steer the minibus, in an only-slightly-wobbly fashion, back out through the turrets and away from the palace.

"Are you *serious*?" she managed to say a moment later. *"We're stealing an enchanted minibus?"*

"Not stealing," said Roxy. "Borrowing."

A grin spread across Jones's face.

"Oh," she said, hauling herself up and staggering over to Roxy. "I am *so* having a go on this thing myself."

It was only now that Roxy realized how much she was shaking. She stood up and let Jones slide into the driver's seat and take the wheel. Then she sat heavily down on the floor beside the gearstick, holding her hairdo for balance.

"Do you think she saw me?"

"Did who see you?" Jones was poking her tongue out in concentration as she lurched the minibus over the tops of the trees.

"That was my sister! The one in the red coat."

"Who, Little Miss Glam-Pants?" Jones raised an

eyebrow. "She's not at all like I imagined her! And talking of people who are nothing like I thought, how awesome are *you*, Roxy Humperdinck? What came over you, suddenly deciding to take on a flying bus like this?"

"Mrs Smith is coming," Roxy explained. "I heard Gretel on the phone. She said Mrs Smith was on her way to the retreat to question Mortadella about the prison breakout." She swallowed, hard. "You know, I don't think my sister really *is* just a loo-cleaner at the Ministry."

"Ah. I see."

This was something, Roxy had to admit, she was kind of loving about Jones. For whatever reason – maybe because she wanted to keep her own life as private as possible – she didn't pry. She took stuff at face value. Which was something Roxy herself was going to have to start doing an awful lot *less*, she realized, if she wasn't going to be totally lied to any more.

"So," Jones went on, "I'm flying this thing back to Rexopolis, right?"

"What?"

"Well, you said you wanted to go home. So we should head back to Rexopolis. Isn't that what you want?"

This, Roxy realized in a shimmering instant, was not what she wanted.

Maybe it was the adrenaline rush from flying a magical minibus. Maybe it was the shock of discovering that her sister was clearly one of MOOOOOH's secret agents. Maybe it was discovering that her family history was way, way more steeped in all this Dark Magic madness than she could ever have imagined.

Or maybe it was that she *was* cut out for saving the world.

And she would never know unless she tried.

"No." Roxy shook her head firmly. "I've changed my mind. I'm coming with you, Jones. We're doing this."

"Woo-hoo!" Jones punched the air with a fist. "All right, then. Let's head north till we hit the McWitch family fortress! Well, not *actually* hit. You know how to land this thing, right?"

"You know," said Roxy, getting to her feet and perching on the side of the driver's seat beside Jones, "I actually think I do."

## 17

"You ring the doorbell."

"No, you ring the doorbell."

"No, *you* ring the doorbell."

"No, *you*… Hang on a sec, QG. *Is* there actually a doorbell?"

"Oh. I hadn't looked. I was distracted by the huge moat."

"Yeah, it's awesome, isn't it?"

"Awesome? Jones, the water is actually *black*."

"Well, that's probably just some trick of the light."

"I don't know if you've noticed, Jones, but there hardly *is* any light. As in, it's almost nightfall. And we're standing outside a witch's fortress. And if you're not scared, why don't *you* ring the doorbell?"

"Because I thought we established there isn't one."

"Well, knock on the door, then!"

"It's not a door. It's a portcullis."

"Then knock on the portcullis!"

"Jeez-Louise, Roxy Humperdinck! I thought you were getting to be less of a cowardly custard, but apparently I was—"

And then a trapdoor opened up beneath them and Jones and Roxy both dropped sharply down into the dungeon below.

## 18

"OK," admitted Jones, "you might have been right about the danger thing."

It had been six terrifying minutes since the two girls had fallen through the secret trapdoor into the pitch-black dungeon.

It had taken Jones and Roxy those entire six minutes to stop yelling and clinging to each other.

"But let's not panic," Jones went on. "Panic will get us nowhere. Panic is for losers."

"Then what do you s-s-s-suggest," asked Roxy, her teeth chattering from a terrible cocktail of cold and fear, "we actually d-d-d-d-do? That trapdoor is too high above us, and d-d-d-didn't you hear the lock click shut as we landed?"

"Hey, I could climb up your hair, maybe, and see if I can reach high enough to pick the lock…

I only wish I hadn't left my kitbag on the minibus," Jones added sorrowfully. "Everything's in there. My lock-picking tools, my torch…"

"T-t-torch! My phone!" Roxy suddenly remembered her phone, and scrabbled in her coat pocket. "And not just a torch! We can use it to c-c-c-call for help."

It was dead. All that navigation to the Fabulous Forest had finished off the battery.

"Pity," said Jones, sounding defeated for a moment. "Nothing else in your pockets? Something that might help me pick a lock? A paperclip? A hairgrip?"

"I've got the minibus keys. Oh, and this stupid giveaway from the Proon Puffs packet…"

Jones felt both the items in the darkness. "Nope, no good. Keys are far too big for a fiddly job like lock-picking. And that triangle rock thing is totally the wrong shape. Do you maybe have a knitting needle? A crochet hook?"

"For heaven's *sake*, Jones, why would I carry a whole bunch of random haberdashery equipment in my pockets?"

"OK, OK … then we'll just have to find another exit." The confidence had returned to Jones's voice. "Trust me, QG, my stepmother used to lock me in a cupboard, sometimes, and…" She stopped. "My point is, nobody ever locks you in somewhere that doesn't have an actual *door*. You think Witchalina McWitch comes in through that trapdoor?"

"Why would she c-c-come in at all?"

"To give us food, water… It'll depend on exactly how long she's planning on keeping us down here. Days or weeks. Or months. *Hopefully* not years…"

"OK, let's look for an exit," said Roxy, feeling a sudden overwhelming need to *stop Jones talking*. "You're right, there has to be a d-d-d-door…"

Fifteen minutes of shuffling-around-in-the-pitch-darkness later, they both had to admit: there was no door.

They sank down, back-to-back, in total silence.

"So," Roxy said in a very, very small voice, "we're not getting home tonight after all, are we?"

"We're not," said Jones. "No."

They fell silent again.

"But seriously, kid," Jones went on, "you can't be worried about getting in trouble with your sister any more! You could stay out all night, every night for months, and she'd have literally *zero right* to get even a bit tetchy."

"It's true." Roxy swallowed. "I can't believe she lied about being a loo-cleaner. I can't believe I *believed* it."

"Yeah. She's clearly a massively elite MOOOOOH agent."

"Massively elite," sighed Roxy.

"With a humble loo-cleaner alias."

"It's a pretty good alias," Roxy admitted.

"So, your brother's a world-famous rock star, your sister's this total super-spy…"

"I don't need to hear again about how ordinary and boring I am, Jones, thank you."

"Hey! I wasn't going to say that." Jones actually sounded rather hurt. "Neither of them has ever tried to save the universe, have they?"

"*Country*, Jones."

"Planet," Jones compromised. "Anyway, are you hungry? I stuffed a couple of Mortadella's vegan muffins in my pocket, right before you pulled me up into the sky. They'll probably be gross but they'll be better than nothing."

"Thanks, Jones. I'm starving." Roxy reached out a hand in the darkness and waved it around until she connected with Jones's. "I could eat a … wow, you *really* could do with some hand lotion."

Jones's hand felt like paper. No: *papyrus*.

"What do you mean?"

"Well, I don't want to be rude, but you should probably take a bit more care of your hands. Put lotion on sometimes? Trim your nails, occasionally?"

"I trim my nails!"

"You clearly don't."

"Well, let's see how great *your* hand-care regime is, shall we?" Jones snapped. "Exactly! Just as I thought. Your nails feel *appalling*. So long they're all curled over, and pointy at the ends … I mean, come on! Introduce yourself to a pair of scissors."

"My nails are super-short! And at least *my* hands aren't so dry they feel all wrinkled, and papery, and…"

Roxy stopped before saying the word *ancient*.

It was just dawning on her that she probably wasn't touching Jones's hand at all.

In the pitch black of the dungeon, the sharp-clawed hand she could feel could have belonged to absolutely anyone.

Someone like…

"Welcome home, dear niece," rasped a creaky, *witchy* voice from beside them.

And then there was a sound like a match being struck.

A face loomed into the match-light.

It was a face with a hooked nose. It was a face with warts. It was a face that was unmistakably green.

"Oh," said the witch in the same creaky rasp, only sounding a bit miffed this time. "Neither of you is my niece."

"I-I…" stuttered Roxy.

"We-we…" stammered Jones.

"Buuuuuut," the witch carried on, her creaky voice turning into a croon, "this is even better. I like meeting new people. Especially girls. With *pretty hair*."

"Th-thanks," Jones gulped. "I dyed it when I ran away. It was meant to be jet black but actually it went this kind of—"

"Not *your* hair!" snapped the witch. She took one of the loose tendrils that had started to tumble down from Roxy's monstrous hair-do. "*This* hair. *So pretty…*"

Then she waved the other hand.

There was a bright green flash and a loud bang, like thunder and lightning striking at the exact same moment.

The next thing Roxy knew, she was sitting on a cold, hard floor in a different room.

And she was completely alone.

## 19

"JONES!" Roxy yelled at the top of her lungs. "JONES, CAN YOU HEAR ME?"

There was no answer.

"JONES!" she shrieked with gut-busting force. "JOOOOOOOOOONES!"

There was still no answer.

"Oh no oh no oh no oh no," babbled Roxy, actually starting to crawl around in a circle on the floor.

Here she was, separated from her only friend, who was presumably still languishing in that horrible dank dungeon, only to end up herself in…

*Oh.*

"In a witch's tower," she said.

She stopped crawling and looked around, properly, at her new surroundings.

There could be no doubt – no doubt whatsoever –

that this was a witch's tower.

The walls were curved, making the room a perfect circle. They were made of crumbled dark-grey rock and were papered with peeling wallpaper featuring patterns of cobwebs and bats. There was a black-velvet sofa scattered with purple cushions embroidered with silvery broomsticks and coppery cauldrons, and beside it there was even an *actual* cauldron, though it was covered in a thick lattice of spider's webs that suggested it hadn't been used in a while. Across the room, a narrow, arched window showed a moonlit view down over the Blizzy Lizzies.

Yep, this was a witch's tower.

This would have been a great discovery if only Jones had been there to discover it with her.

A sound from behind made Roxy jump.

"Pretty, pretty…" It was the bone-chilling croon again. "Such a pretty head of hair."

The voice was coming from behind the only door.

"Hey!" Roxy leaped to her feet, strode to the door and banged on it. "Stop spying on me! And stop talking about my hair! And, more to the point, LET ME OUT!"

"Pretty, pretty," was the witch's sing-song reply. "Blonde and lovely."

"I said, stop it!" Roxy thumped the door again. "And tell me where Jones is!"

"Perfect golden tresses," went on the witch. "A waterfall of blondeness!"

Roxy stopped banging.

She had heard that expression before.

*Just one more thing, you'll need LONG hair – a waterfall of blondeness…*

It was from the rhyming newspaper ad that had led her to the storage vault in the first place.

But the ad hadn't been placed by Witchalina McWitch. It had been placed by a Trixie T McWitch.

The witch on the other side of the door wasn't Mortadella's friend Witchalina, but another witch entirely. Trixie T McWitch, perhaps. And who knew how much good *she* had in her?

"Look." Roxy tried to keep her voice level. "My sister works for the Ministry Overseeing, Organizing or Occasionally Opposing Hocus-Pocus. When she finds out you've kidnapped me, she'll turn up with … with … the very latest in anti-witch weaponry," she improvised. "Now will you let me go?"

There was silence from the other side of the door.

Then, "Pretty, pretty…" came the familiar sing-song as the witch's retreating voice faded away to nothing.

Roxy took a deep breath. Then she put her hands on her hips and said, "OK. Let's get this show on the road."

Then she gazed about the tower room, wondering where *this show* might start.

"*For the stone with all the power,*" she murmured, "*seek within a witch's tower. Have a look around the place; you'll find the answer in your face.*"

*In. Your. Face.*

Even as she thought this, a face caught her eye.

It was her own, and it was gazing palely back at her from a small, oval, rather tarnished mirror on the adjacent wall.

*In. Your. Face.*

"I wonder," she breathed.

She stepped closer to the mirror.

"Is this," she murmured, "the answer to the riddle?"

"It is," came a voice.

Roxy screamed.

The voice was coming from the mirror.

## 20

"Well done!" the voice declared. "You've cracked the code. Your two and two make four!"

Roxy stared at the mirror.

The mirror – or rather, her face in it – stared back at her.

She reached out a hand.

"I hope you've washed those mucky mitts," the mirror snapped, "since crawling on the floor."

"I ... er..." stammered Roxy.

"Good hygiene is important," continued the mirror, "and I do not care for grime. If *I* had hands, you grubby girl, *I'd* wash them all the time."

Roxy peered more closely at the mirror. It was pretty unremarkable-looking: that tarnished frame surrounding plain glass. It did not have eyes. It did not have a mouth. In fact, it was impossible to see *how* it was talking.

But there could be absolutely no mistaking the fact that it *was*.

"I'd treat myself to bubble baths," the mirror went on, dreamily, "to get off all the gunge. And if I found a grease-spot, I would scrub it with a sponge. I'd use a lovely scented soap – I'm fond of rose and lily – and after that, I'd—"

"Sorry," interrupted Roxy, "but are you speaking in … uh … *rhyme*?"

"Why?" asked the mirror, sounding hurt. "Are you implying I sound silly?"

"Oh, no! Not at all," said Roxy hastily. "You sound … er … quite lovely."

"How nice of you to say!" said the mirror. "How kind. Your manners are exquisite. Now, tell me, pray, the reason for this unexpected visit."

"Well," said Roxy, after a moment. "Your … owner? Trixie, the creepy green-skinned witch? She's kind of locked me up. I think it's all something to do with … wanting my hair?"

"Oh dear," the mirror sighed. "I do apologize for Trixie's naughty tricks. She's pulled these kinds of crazy stunts since eighteen thirty-six."

"Good thing it wasn't a year earlier," said Roxy,

"or that would never have rhymed!"

There was a short, rather peevish silence from the mirror.

"I hope that you're not making fun," it said. "I hope that you're not mocking..."

"No, not at all!" said Roxy. She added quickly, "In fact, as magic mirrors go, I think you're really rocking!"

This time the mirror's silence was longer.

"OK, OK," said Roxy, holding up her hands. "I won't try that again."

"I'd rather that," said the mirror, before muttering, "and by the way, *your* rhyme was truly shocking."

"So it sounds like you've been around this place a while," Roxy said. "And you say Trixie has trapped girls in here before. Tell me: how do they *usually* get out?"

"Dear Witchalina – Trixie's niece – she solves the situation," the mirror replied. "But Witchalina isn't here. She's on a nice vacation."

"Witchalina is Trixie's niece? And she normally sets the girls free? And she's ON HOLIDAY?"

Roxy ran to the narrow window. With some effort, she could probably squeeze through it. But *then* what? It was a hundred metres down to the icy blackness of the moat. Who knew how deep that was? And what *lurked* in there...

189

"With very deep regret, dear girl," began the mirror, "I'll tell you what I know. There's simply no way out of here. Believe me. Have a go. That window's not an option: it is too far from the ground. You're welcome to try shouting but there's nobody around…"

"I get the point!" Roxy's heart sank. "I guess I'm… stuck here, then."

"Unless," the mirror said eagerly, "you know a useful prince? Now wouldn't that be dandy? That clever girl Rapunzel made darn sure *she* had one handy."

"Wait – this was *Rapunzel's* tower?"

"Well, locking up blonde girlies is a proud McWitch tradition. It's only Witchalina who does not share this ambition."

Roxy began to laugh, rather hysterically.

"Let me get this straight. I'm shut up in *Rapunzel's* tower. My brother and sister are *Hansel and Gretel*. And you're probably, I don't know, Snow White's stepmother's mirror, or something…"

"I certainly am *not*!" the mirror gasped. "*That* mirror's nasty through and through!"

"Really? I thought it was just honest, and told evil Queen Bellissima what it thought of her."

The mirror snorted. "It merely spoke the truth, as magic mirrors *have* to do. We cannot utter falsehoods and we never simply flatter. We have to point out

190

massive zits and whether you've got fatter. We cannot fail to tell you if your nose takes too much space. And most of us will help you make improvements to your face. But Snow White's stepmum's mirror played a rather different game—"

"Look ... Mirror," Roxy interrupted. "Can I call you Mirror, by the way?"

"You're kidding." The mirror sounded stunned. "Are you *serious?* I've never had a *name.*"

"Mirror, I have a question," Roxy went on. "Have you ever heard of the Witching Stones?"

Mirror sucked in its breath. "Oh me, oh my," it breathed. "I can't recall when last I heard *them* mentioned."

"Well, I'm interested in the Seventh Witching Stone. The most powerful one of all. Can you tell me anything more about it? Most important of all, where it might be hidden?"

"Of course! I'd be delighted, dear. I'm very well-intentioned!"

Roxy blinked. "Wait – it's *that easy?*"

"There's just one teeny caveat: the password. Do you know it?"

"There's a password?"

"Why, yes, of course! Oh, dearie me. I hope that doesn't blow it?"

"Password…" Roxy's forehead knitted. "All we found in *Mrs Tabitha* was the clue. If it's a password you need, I'll … ow!"

Something had hit her on the back of the neck.

It had just flown in through the narrow arched window behind her.

"Attackers!" shrieked Mirror. "Fierce marauders! Quick! Prepare the boiling water! Then chuck it out the window! Don't surrender! Give no quarter!"

"Who in their right mind would *attack* a witch's tower?" Roxy clambered up onto the velvet sofa to get a better view out of the window.

In the thin moonlight, on the ground far below, she could just see…

"Jones! It's you!"

"Of course it's blooming me!" Jones yelled, through cupped hands. She was standing on the other side of the murky black moat. "I've been down here yelling your name for the last three minutes. I was just about to go and fetch the minibus and fly up, but then I remembered: you're the one with the keys, right?"

"Right. Sorry, I was just chatting to … er … someone. Are you all right?" Roxy called back. "Where's Trixie?"

"Trixie?"

"The witch!"

"I thought she was called Witchalina!"

"No, Witchalina's away. *This* one's her auntie, Trixie."

"Whoever she is, she's fast asleep at the kitchen table," Jones yelled. "Well, I say *fast asleep* … I may have sort of kind of ever-so-slightly hit her on the head with a frying-pan."

*"Jones!"*

"Hey, she brought it on herself. She got me out of that dungeon and started ordering me around the kitchen like some kind of servant. And I'm not being anybody's servant ever again, even if I wasn't on a mission to save the world!"

"Good for you, Jones, but focus, please! How do I get out of here?"

"Don't worry. I've got a great plan." Jones cleared her throat. "Roxy, Roxy, let down your hair!"

Roxy stared down at her.

"Come on, it's obvious! *Let down your hair!* That's what fair maidens do when they're stuck up a tower. It worked for Rapunzel!"

Roxy patted the hideous hair-do. She didn't feel much like a fair maiden, but there was a *lot* of hair in there.

"OK, but I don't even know *if* it'll come down."

"Just give it a try! And you'll have to give it a

massive swing when you chuck it out, so it reaches this side of the moat."

With difficulty, Roxy reached up and began disentangling the huge quantity of hairpins, grips and clips that Frankie had somehow magicked into the hairdo. The hair itself felt incredibly heavy as she looped it into a kind of lasso and then – with some effort – shoved it through the window.

It was only at the very last second that she realized she should have grabbed onto something. The weight of all that hair was going to topple her out of the window too. Thinking fast, she stuck one foot deep down the side of the sofa and clung on to the fragment of tattered curtain for dear life.

It worked. She stayed put.

"They never mentioned that in *Rapunzel*," she gasped.

Several painful, scalp-pulling minutes later, Jones's face appeared at the window. She pulled herself through before collapsing, red-faced and breathless and still minus her left boot, onto the sofa.

"I'll tell you what, kid," she puffed when she could talk. "I have new respect for any prince that's done this. It's a lot harder than…"

She stopped.

"Bellissima's balaclava." She was scrambling to her

feet. "Is this the place? Is this *the* tower?"

"Yes, and Jones…"

Jones whooped. "OK, we have to start looking for the clue. *Have a look around the place; you'll find the answer in your face…*"

"Yes, Jones, I've already…"

"I'll bet it's something to do with this grotty-looking mirror right here," Jones said, striding towards Mirror. "And this being fairytale stuff, we're probably supposed to say something like, I dunno, *Mirror, Mirror on the wall, who's the fairest of them all?* And then, if mirrors could actually talk, the mirror would reply—"

"I do not like your tone," said Mirror haughtily. "I don't take kindly to your teasing. And OMG, those eyebrows! Have you never heard of tweezing?"

Jones's mouth dropped open. "You seriously *talk*?"

"Don't ask it a question!" Roxy begged, but it was too late.

"I do indeed," replied Mirror. "I talk. I speak. I comment and I chat. I give my views. I pass remarks on this and sometimes that. I like a good old chinwag, I enjoy a good debate—"

"Right, I get the point. No need to hammer it home."

"AND BEING INTERRUPTED IS A THING I REALLY HATE!" Mirror yelled.

"Is it talking in actual *rhyme*?" Jones hissed at Roxy.

195

Roxy nodded. "You said yourself, that's how they all spoke in the Cursed Kingdom. Anyway, it's definitely the thing the clue was pointing us to. It knows about the Stone. But it says it can't tell us anything without a password."

"Right," said Jones, grabbing it off the wall. "Look, Mirror," she went on pleasantly, "as it happens, we don't have a moment to waste working out some password. The future of our planet is at stake. So what about these words instead? *Shatter. Shards. Smithereens.* Get it?"

Mirror let out a little shriek. "You brute! You cannot threaten me! Oh, what a nasty thug!"

"She didn't mean to upset you…" Roxy began.

"Too late for that!" sniffed Mirror. "I'm shaken up. I rather need a hug."

"Hey, we can all talk about our feelings some other time –" Jones rolled her eyes – "but for now, just answer me this, Mirror. Do you remember the bad old days of the Perpetual Wickedness?"

Mirror was – astonishingly – silent, which was enough of an answer to Jones's question.

"Because there's a real danger of all that Dark Magic being unleashed again," Jones continued, "if we don't find the Seventh Stone before Queen Bellissima does. She's escaped from prison, you see – well, her spirit has – and—"

"Forget that silly password!" Mirror gasped. "I will tell you all I know! It happened here, right in this tower, a long, long time ago. Some magic folk enchanted me (it's kind of what they do), and gave me just one purpose: I'm the Keeper of a Clue."

Mirror paused. When it next spoke, its voice was low.

"Tick-tock, goes the clock. I hope you're feeling plucky. This time, I've got your number and it isn't very lucky."

Jones frowned.

"That's *it*? Another blooming rhyme?"

"Not *my* problem!" huffed Mirror. "My job's just to give the information. *You're* the ones who need to find the proper explanation!"

"I know the answer," said Roxy suddenly.

Jones turned to look at her.

"I know what the clue means." Roxy sounded as dumbstruck as she felt.

Because the clue could only mean one thing.

The Witching Stone was hidden in a clock.

A clock that had something to do with an unlucky number.

"It's in the Dodgy Old Clock," she said. "In Minister Splendid's office. It must have been there all along. Right in the heart of the Soup Ministry."

## 21

"So you're absolutely sure," Jones asked, for the dozenth time, "that this Dodgy Old Clock is *thirteen* minutes fast?"

"Absolutely sure," said Roxy, also for the dozenth time.

It had been several hours since both girls, and Mirror, had made it out of the tower. Jones, clutching a thrilled Mirror (tucked inside one of the velvet cushions for safety), had used Roxy's hair for the descent before flying the enchanted minibus up to collect Roxy herself. The overnight minibus flight back to Rexopolis had been rather slow and bumpy – they suspected it needed some sort of magical recharge, as they seemed to be flying at half the speed of their first flight – and the dawn walk from where they'd left the bus, with its **INVISIBILITY SHIELD** on, in a lay-by on the edge of the city, had been freezing. (Jones had been eager to fly the bus all the way into the city but Roxy, concerned about what might happen if the **INVISIBILITY SHIELD** pinged itself off for any reason, had won that disagreement.) They were exhausted and hungry. The stale goji-berry-and-bran muffin they'd shared during the turbulent flight had been rock-hard and so truly foul-tasting that even Jones had given up chewing her half of it after a few mouthfuls.

The *only* piece of good news was that, for once, one of Frankie's spells had done what it was supposed to do. Shortly after taking off from the McWitch Fortress – in fact exactly as Jones's watch had beeped midnight – Roxy's hideous heap of hair had disappeared. She could not say that she missed it. And it was a relief that it had disappeared before their return to Rexopolis, because they did *not* want to draw undue attention to themselves. Especially not as, back here in the city, there were *even more* **SMOG** patrols than normal, particularly around the Ministry. This was where the girls were now, making their way towards the staff quarters.

"And you're sure it's kept inside the Minister's study?" Jones asked.

"For the last time, I'm sure!" Roxy was too tired for the barrage of questions, particularly when – as far as she was concerned – their mission was pretty much over. "Jones, seriously, can we not just crash and sleep now? I thought you agreed, back there on the bus, that if the Stone is safe in the Ministry – and must have been for *years*, by the way – then there's nothing left for us to do. Queen Bellissima won't be able to get her hands on it there."

"Oh, come on. If *I* managed to break into the Ministry, how hard do you think it would be for old Bellissima? She's a *spirit*. She can get in *anywhere*. Through an *open window*. Via the *ventilation shafts*."

"And what do you suggest *we* could do with the Stone if we pinched it from the Clock? Take it somewhere more secure? How would we even do that? Pop along to the Royal Palace, charm our way past the armed guards and ask Queen Ariadne if she's got any room among the Crown Jewels?"

"Look, I don't know, all right?" Jones had been less buoyant than usual since the jump from the tower; deflated, almost. "I just … I just want to *see* the Stone. I've been thinking about finding it – dreaming about finding it – ever since I first discovered Dad's notebooks. And we've come such a long way. It feels wrong not to see it all the way to the end."

"I understand that, Jones, I really do. But breaking into the Minister's office… You got incredibly lucky last time. And don't forget, most of the **SMOGs** were guarding the Ministry ballroom that night, not the Minister's office. Look at all the extra **SMOGs** around today. They're everywhere!"

"Trust me, I've noticed." Jones was pulling her fedora low as they approached the Soup Minister's Residence. "But you know what, I'll just bet they've been way too busy organizing all the obvious defences – doors, windows, ventilation shafts – that they've forgotten all about boarding up the old underground tunnel. And even if they haven't, that needn't stop us! I've got some *very* nifty equipment in here." She patted her remarkable kitbag confidently.

"Look, I really hope you're right," Roxy sighed. "I want to see this through just as much as—"

A loud cough came from inside the cushion.

"What is it, Mirror?" she added in a whisper. "Are you all right?"

"No, not at all," came Mirror's muffled voice. "I'm bored in here. I really want to *see*! If you'd been stuck indoors for years, you'd feel the same as me."

"I can't get you out," Roxy whispered apologetically. "There are **SMOGs** all over the place."

"Basically, put a sock in it, Mr Mirror," Jones added. "Now, do we need to get past those guards," she asked Roxy, nodding at the dozen huge **SMOGs** that blocked the front doors, "or is there another way to get to your sister's place?"

"Don't worry, the Staff Quarters are totally separate," said Roxy, steering Jones away from the grand main entrance and all the way round to the back, where the plain-brick staff flats were. "I seriously doubt they've bothered to put anyone... *Oh*."

There was a **SMOG** guarding the entrance to the Staff Quarters.

He was **SMOG**-style huge, **SMOG**-style armed and as grim-faced as any **SMOG** Roxy had ever seen.

"We'll never get past him without a pass," Roxy hissed as the girls darted behind the nearest tree trunk.

"What pass?"

"Security passes that get you into all the buildings in the Ministry. My sister has one but I don't. Usually we don't *need* one, but if they've put a guard there..."

"Hey, I've got this." Jones was already reaching into her kitbag and pulling out what was left of her half of the foul-tasting goji-berry-and-bran muffin. "See, *this* is why you never throw food away, even the revolting stuff," she went on, drawing back one arm. "An *inedible* muffin might just make an *incredible* weapon..."

She threw the hard muffin-lump, fast and with

202

unerring accuracy, right at the **SMOG**'s face.

He shrieked and clasped both hands to his rather large nose. Red liquid gushed. Either the goji berries had been a lot juicier than they'd looked, or that was one impressive nosebleed.

Jones stuck up a thumb in satisfaction as the **SMOG**, presumably in search of wadding for his nose, staggered off.

"Works every time," she whispered.

Fleetingly, Roxy wondered if, just maybe, Jones had pulled this kind of move before. If this might in fact have anything to do with the Cupcake Incident she wouldn't speak about...

"Let's go!" Jones went on, nipping out from behind the tree and pulling Roxy with her. "He could be back any moment!"

Roxy's heart was hammering as she led Jones through the unguarded doors, then all the way along the empty corridor to Gretel's bedsit. This door was locked, of course – Gretel was always security-conscious – but Roxy had her key. As she rooted around her pocket for it, her fingers brushed against the educational toy from the Proon Puffs packet. Was that *still* in there? She thought she might have dropped it back in Trixie's dungeon. She'd chuck it out later, but right now she just wanted to get the two of them safely into the room without being spotted.

She held her breath as she turned the key in the lock, half wondering if Gretel might be here, but it was all clear.

"Right. The bathroom!" Jones announced, striding towards the bathroom door and pushing it open. "So, where's this tunnel entrance, then?"

Her heart in her mouth, Roxy knelt down beside the bath and jiggled the side panel. It came loose just as easily as before, and as she pulled it away, half expecting to see nothing but boards – or worse: *bricks* – relief surged through her.

"Ha! Just as I thought!" crowed Jones as the stone steps appeared before them. "They haven't boarded it up yet!" She leaned down to peer into the darkness. "Awe …" she breathed. "… some."

"Come on," Roxy said, sliding limbo-style under the top edge of the bath, lowering her bottom onto the top step and then bumping her way down five or six more steps until she could stand. "You don't mind small, cramped spaces, do you, Jones?" she called over her shoulder.

"Kid." Jones was following close behind. "I hunt for ancient artefacts. You don't get far in that game if you suffer from claustrophobia… *Wow*," she finished as she straightened up and took the last few stairs at a jog to join Roxy on the slippery stone floor. "So this is the Ministry labyrinth!"

"Labyrinth?" Roxy suddenly remembered that Jones had used this exact word the night they had met in the vault. "Wait, how many tunnels are there, exactly?"

"Dozens of 'em! Hundreds, for all I know. Dad's notes say the Ministry was built on top of the site of the Cursed Kingdom's Royal Palace. The old, creepy one Queen Bellissima would have lived in, not the nice, clean, shiny one Queen Ariadne lives in now, across the Square." Jones's voice echoed off the damp walls. "Can you just *imagine* how much magical skulduggery went on down here all those years ago? And then when they razed it all to the ground as part of the Great Clean-Up, they kept the tunnels open so that anything BOBI-related could still be kept down here, out of sight. No wonder your sister ended up with one of the best entrances, her being one of Minister Splendid's top agents, and all that."

"You OK there, Mirror?" Roxy suddenly asked, at a loud moan from inside the cushion. "Don't tell me *you're* claustrophobic?"

"Alas," wailed Mirror, "if only *that* was what was setting me a-quiver! I cannot say the cause, but *something's* causing me to shiver..."

"Oh, get a grip, will you?" Jones was already setting off into the blackness. "There's no room on this mission for scaredy-cats. Wow, this is *dark*. I'll just grab my torch."

"It's OK, Mirror," Roxy said as she followed Jones. "It's not far to the vault, and from there we can get up into the Minister's office, find the Clock, have a quick look at the Stone … we'll be right back here again ten, maybe fifteen minutes from now!" she finished, more confidently than she felt. "Mission accomplished. There's really nothing to be scared—"

"AAAAAAAAAAAAAAAAAAAAAAAAAAGH!" shrieked Jones. Her torch and her hat clattered to the cobbles. "YOU DIDN'T TELL ME THERE WERE SPIDERS!"

"It's an old tunnel six metres underground," said Roxy. "I didn't think I *had* to."

"Maybe, but you could have mentioned there'd be MASSIVE ones!" Jones scrabbled for the torch. "With hairy legs! And … and fangs!"

"Spiders don't have fangs."

"This one did! And it had a really *evil* look on its face, too." Jones shuddered.

"Jones, are you *scared* of spiders?"

"Hey! I'm not scared of anything! I mean, find me a spider right now, and I'll stand right up to it. Show it who's boss. AAAAAAAAAAAAAAAAGH!" Jones shrieked a second time, grabbing Roxy's arm. "There it was again!"

Deep inside the cushion, Mirror emitted a loud snigger. "Correct me if I've got it wrong," it said with rich satisfaction. "My hearing's not the best. But wasn't there *no room for scaredy-cats* upon this quest?"

"Now, listen to me, you jumped-up household—"

"Jones, come on. The longer we take, the greater the chance of getting caught. So why don't you put your hat back on –" Roxy grabbed Jones's fedora from the floor and shoved it at her – "and lead the way for once? That way, I can take the full force of any skull-burrowing spiders."

The walk through the chilly, dank tunnel seemed longer than Roxy had remembered it. This, she had no doubt, was entirely down to Jones. Every drip of slimy water from over their heads, every hint of cobweb caused a full-blown panic attack. Roxy was relieved to finally be able to whisper, "We're here!" as they reached the end of the tunnel.

"I'd thought we'd never make it," gasped Jones, shoving past Roxy to be the first to scramble up through the gap high in the wall. "OK, as soon as we get into the vault," she added, "I want a proper check-over. I'm absolutely certain there's *something* in my hair and… Oh."

Because they hadn't come out into the vault. They must have taken a wrong turn in the tunnels.

They had come out into Bijou Splendid's bedroom.

To be more accurate, they had come out through a fireplace grate that – just like the one in Minister Splendid's office – was totally and utterly fake.

The huge bedroom loomed, pink and sparkly, around them.

"Wrong turn." Roxy was already edging back down through the fake fireplace. "Let's take it a bit slower this time. Maybe we should go back to where we started, and I can try to remember the way I went the first time."

But Jones was not following her.

Jones was, instead, staring at the ornate antique dressing table.

"Wow," she breathed. "This thing is incredible."

"It's pink," said Roxy flatly. "And glittery. And hideous."

"But it's *so old*. It's absolutely *fascinating*…"

"This is no time to get obsessed by another of your ancient artifacts…"

Jones was not listening. She was walking towards the dressing table as if drawn by an invisible thread.

"Jones, come *on*—"

Roxy was interrupted by the sound of a blood-curdling moan from inside the cushion.

"Mirror?" She reached in and grabbed it. "Are you OK?"

"Oh, Roxy," gasped Mirror, "there is once again an *icky* feeling dawning. There's something *evil* in this place! Please, Roxy, heed my warning!"

Roxy was struggling to keep her patience, both with Mirror and with Jones. "I'll be happy to heed your warning *after* we're safely back in my sister's room. Jones, *please*," she added, "will you just hurry?"

"I can't be certain what it is," Mirror was saying now, "but something in this room is filling me with fear and dread and quite a lot of doom. I'm feeling really, *really* freaked! It's making me quite weepy! There's *something here*! I'm getting chills! This place is proper creepy."

It was a fair point. Bijou's bedroom *was* a bit creepy, Roxy had to admit, what with all the pink teddies on the frilly four-poster bed, and the full-sized photos of Bijou all over the walls, and the ghastly pink-painted antique mirror above the dressing table Jones was acting so loopy over...

Well, that was strange.

The ghastly pink-painted antique mirror.

It wasn't pink any more.

The whole thing, glass and frame and all, had turned very, very black.

## 22

"Uh, Mirror," said Roxy, in a very, very, very quiet voice. "There's something I think you should see."

She edged back up out of the fireplace grate and lifted Mirror so it was facing the black dressing-table mirror over her shoulder.

"Don't freak out," she whispered, "but is, um, *that* the evil thing you're talking about?"

Mirror looked at the other, black mirror.

It took a deep breath.

"THAT'S IT!!!" it yelled, in the most freaking-out way possible. "THAT'S IT! THE EVIL THING! YOU SEE, I WASN'T LYING! THAT'S SNOW WHITE'S STEPMUM'S MIRROR, AND IT'S PROPER TERRIFYING!"

Roxy felt a shudder down her own spine at the sheer terror in Mirror's voice.

"You mean the mirror that always told Queen Bellissima she was the fairest of them all?" she asked.

"Exactly! And I promise you, this dark glass can't be trusted. It's lain in wait for decades, since Bellissima combusted." Mirror lowered its voice to a whisper. "Now listen, Roxy, dearest girl: I know I'm sounding stressed. But trust me when I say, I think that mirror is … *possessed*."

"How quaint," came a sudden voice from the other, dark mirror. It was silken and female, and low. "How sweet. How nice to hear an uncorrupted mind! But heed that little looking-glass. It's right, I think you'll find."

Roxy was just thinking, *Oh no, not another rhyming mirror,* when she realized she had a bigger problem on her hands.

Jones was looking, quite simply, *zombified*.

"Jones?" Roxy grabbed her by the shoulders, staring into glassy eyes. "Jones, are you –" She was about to say *all right* but something made her finish, instead, with – *"there?"*

"The Dark Glass has enchanted her!" gasped Mirror. "And I've a nasty hunch … that Jones's normal thinking skills have toddled off to lunch."

"I'm glad to say," purred the Dark Glass, "that yes, indeed, she's joined my little band. She gives me what

I do not have: to wit, a useful hand. For I am just a piece of glass; I cannot work alone." The Dark Glass's silken voice twisted into a serpentine hiss directed at Jones. "My queen requires her heart's desire: *the precious Seventh Stone.*"

Jones took three stiff steps closer to the Dark Glass.

"Jones," said Roxy, her heart racing. "If you're messing around, stop. Stop *now*. This is freaky…"

"You know who dwells inside me now," the Dark Glass murmured to Jones. "I see it in your eyes."

"I do," intoned Jones, in a voice as zombified as her walk. "It's Queen Bellissima, the powerful and wise."

"OK," Roxy whispered to Mirror. "Good call on the whole *possessed* thing."

The Dark Glass hissed at Roxy, "*Possessed* is not a word I like, I'd rather it was ditched. I prefer a finer term … perhaps let's say *bewitched*. Two decades I have waited for my dreams to come to pass. Just now, my queen returned at last; she shelters in my glass!"

So they had only been a few moments behind Queen Bellissima! If she hadn't been so terrified, Roxy would have been immensely proud.

"And – praise to Diabolica – the Stone shall set her free," the evil mirror continued. "Now, girlie," it went on, addressing Jones again, "*fetch that Witching Stone and bring it here to me.*"

Jones nodded robotically and turned to the door of the bedroom.

"Jones!" Roxy tried to grab her arm, but she brushed it off. "Please, you have to listen to *me*. You're stronger than this! You're better than this! Well, OK, you're definitely *stronger*…" Realizing it was hopeless, she turned back to the Dark Glass. "Let me go instead."

The Dark Glass said nothing in reply for a moment. It simply glittered at her, more blackly than ever.

"I'm the only one who knows how to open the Dodgy Old Clock," fibbed Roxy, hoping she sounded more convincing than she felt. "It's … it's got all these clever locks, you see, and I'm pretty good at lockpicking. Excellent, in fact! Way better than Jones."

Still the Dark Glass said nothing.

Then Roxy felt a horrible sensation, right between the eyes, as though somebody had got hold of her brain and was attempting to pull it out through her forehead. It was, in fact, almost exactly same sensation she'd felt just yesterday, back in Mortadella's office, but this time it wasn't a pleasant feeling. It was positively excruciating. "Stop!" she gasped. "Whatever you're doing … please … stop!"

Just as suddenly as it had started, the pulling, twisting sensation stopped.

"You are immune – how very strange, despite all of my trying," murmured the Dark Glass thoughtfully. "I cannot get inside your head to see if you are lying."

"I'm not lying," lied Roxy. She stared directly at the Dark Glass. "I can open the Clock. I have to be the one to go. Not Jones."

There was another long silence.

"Agreed," the Dark Glass hissed. "Then you may toddle off and bring me back the Stone. And dear Miss Jones can stay with me. I *hate* to be alone."

Roxy had never recognized a threat more clearly in her life.

If she did not bring the Witching Stone back, Jones was in danger.

The kind of danger that made the danger back in Trixie's dungeon look like a fabulous birthday party, complete with face-painting and rainbow cake.

"OK," Roxy declared. "I'll do what you want. I'll get the Stone. But only if you absolutely, one hundred per cent, *cast-iron guarantee* that once I've given it to you, you'll let Jones go." She shuddered at Jones's glassy eyes and empty expression. "You have to … give her back to me."

"You have my word," slithered the Dark Glass. "I'll set her free. Now hurry, girl, and go. I'll give you … seven minutes, tops. You'd better not be slow."

"I'm going!" Roxy reached out to give Jones's icy hand a quick squeeze. "I'll be as fast as I can," she told her.

Then, holding Mirror tightly, she scrambled back through the fake fireplace and down into the pitch-black tunnel.

**23**

Without Jones's torch, the tunnel was blacker than ever. Roxy had to feel her way, a hand on each of the damp walls, and just hope she would notice any fork in the path when she reached it. And that she would take the right one this time. They had seven minutes. Six and a half, now. There was no time for mistakes. The tunnel began to feel more familiar … the walls less damp … the puddles underfoot drying out…

"I think we're here!" she suddenly hissed to Mirror. "The entrance to the vault!"

She put her hands against the wall, felt around and was relieved to feel the gap that she'd gone through last time. She pushed herself through, into the vault itself. Here she had to rely on her memory to get across it in the darkness, but felt her way successfully to the stone steps Jones had sprinted up that first night they had met.

"OK," she murmured. "Now we just have to hope – *really* hope – there's nobody in Minister Splendid's office. Like, any **SMOGs**. Or Minister Splendid himself. Or my sister, pretending to clean his private toilet as part of her deep-cover…"

She reached up and pulled herself through the hole. It was tighter than she had thought. She pushed gently but firmly on the bit of wood in front of her. Please, *please* let this be the right fake fireplace…

Her heart leaped when the thin wooden door popped open, leaving her crawling through another fireplace into the dazzling daylight.

The room was empty! Roxy could have danced for joy, but this wasn't the time.

"Clock," she muttered, gazing around. "Dodgy Old Clock…"

The office was, she couldn't help noticing, almost as ghastly as Bijou's bedroom. This was mostly because there were photos of Minister Splendid *everywhere*: Minister Splendid on horseback; Minister Splendid gazing into the distance on a golf course; Minister Splendid beaming toothily as he chinked champagne glasses with a rather weary-looking Queen Ariadne.

But there, beneath a photo of Minister Splendid winning a cycle race, was an elaborate gold desk.

And on the desk sat a dodgy-looking old clock.

It was a wooden carriage clock, about the size of a small shoebox. The wood – cherry, perhaps, or a light mahogany – was scuffed in places, and the clock face itself was battered.

It was running thirteen minutes fast.

Roxy checked her watch: twenty-one minutes past ten. The Dodgy Old Clock was displaying twenty-six minutes to eleven.

"This is it!" She held it up to the light that poured through the windows, and studied it. "Mirror, I don't suppose you know how to get *into* the clock? Does the back come off, or is there a hidden panel at the bottom?"

"I've not a clue," said Mirror. "But here's a thought: we're in a massive hurry. So bash it open on the desk – all sorted! Bosh! No worry!"

"I'm not going to *bash it open*!" Roxy turned the clock over, but there was nothing to indicate it could open. "I should never have lied about being an expert lock-picker! Jones would know how to get into it!"

"Now listen, dear," said Mirror. "Believe me, you are smarter than you think. Remember that it's *Jones* who, at the present, cannot blink. The queen and her dark mirror couldn't take control of *you*. So take a moment, Roxy, and you'll work out what to do," it finished kindly.

It was such a shock hearing Mirror *not panic* for once that Roxy actually listened.

She found herself taking a deep breath and closing her eyes, the way she always did to clear her mind when she was about to pull her memory trick.

And then something occurred to her.

"What happens," she murmured, "if I just … set the correct time?"

Gently, so as not to damage the clock face, she reached for the minute hand and eased it back … eleven … twelve … thirteen minutes.

For a moment, nothing happened.

Then there was the faintest *click* as the clock face sprang, lightly, open.

Inside the clock was a crevice the shape of a spindly isosceles triangle. And it was completely empty.

"It's not there," Roxy whispered.

"Not *there*?" Mirror was sounding panicked again. "That simply cannot be! The clue was quite specific! Oh, Roxy, Roxy, Roxy, this is properly horrific…"

Roxy stared at the clock, her heart feeling just as empty as that triangle. So she'd been wrong. Mirror's clue must have been talking about something else, another clock, probably, or maybe she'd misunderstood entirely and…

That triangle shape, though.

Roxy frowned, and gazed at it more closely. It was weirdly familiar. She put her fingertip into the groove and ran it down, along and back up the sides of the little triangle. It even *felt* familiar, if it were possible for a small empty isosceles triangle shape to feel familiar.

And then, quite suddenly, she knew.

She knew that exact triangle, its size and its contours, because she'd seen and touched and held that exact triangle before.

"It's all right," she said, above Mirror's wailing. "It's OK. Because you see, Mirror, I've actually got the Stone. I've had it all along, I just didn't realize."

She reached deep into her jacket pocket and felt for the pointless educational toy from the Proon Puffs packet.

She pulled it out, put Mirror down on the desk, and placed the slim isosceles triangle shape into the spindly isosceles triangle-shaped slot in the back of the clock.

She already knew that it would be a perfect fit.

"You *had it in your pocket*?" Mirror said. "How the heck did you not *know*?"

"I thought it was a free giveaway from a cereal packet," Roxy mumbled. Her head ached with the impossibility of trying to figure out this crazy, *crazy* turn of events. "I've literally no idea what it was doing in the Proon Puffs."

"You know what," interrupted Mirror, "tell me later, 'cos we really have to go."

"Yes. Of course." Roxy deftly edged the Stone back out of the clock and held on to it tightly.

And then she picked up Mirror, ran for the fireplace and scrambled back into the vault.

## 24

"Now, Roxy: listen, hear me," Mirror began, its voice jumpy from being bounced up and down as Roxy pelted along the dark tunnel. "We cannot give up the Stone! Bellissima is bad enough when *not* completely grown! Her powers will come flooding back; she'll overthrow the city! And after that, who knows? But rest assured, it won't be..."

There was a loud thud as Roxy ran smack into someone coming the other way along the tunnel.

"... pretty," finished Mirror feebly from the shallow puddle into which it had fallen.

"What...?" Roxy mumbled, her head smarting. "Who...?"

"Oh my stars, I'm *so* sorry," came a voice in the darkness as someone began to help her to her feet. "I didn't see you there! Well, obviously I didn't, because it's so dark down here, and I need my glasses…"

"*Frankie?*" exclaimed Roxy, just able to make out his familiar face. "Is it really you?"

"Oh, my dear child!" Frankie gasped, and gathered her to where his bosom would have been if he hadn't – still – been trapped in the body of a ten-year-old boy. "What in heaven's name are you doing down here?"

"I could ask you the same question!"

"I'm looking for Skinny, of course."

"Skinny's down here too?"

"Yes. *Somewhere.* They brought us both here yesterday, straight from Sector Seven, and they left us in the cells guarded by some *extremely uncivil* **SMOGs**. So when the one guarding me had to go and find a first-aid kit for his friend – I think he'd been punched in the nose or something – I decided enough was enough. I'm on the run, dearie!" Frankie let out a hoot of excitement. "Now, if you could help me track down Skinny's cell… Hold on. Where's my goddaughter?"

"If Jones is whom you speak of, then she's in a sorry state," yelled Mirror from its puddle. "We have to go and save her, and we're running blooming late!"

"Who on earth said that?" Frankie looked around, astonished.

"This talking mirror," said Roxy, grabbing first Mirror and then Frankie's hand. "I'll explain later. But

Jones is in a sorry state, Frankie, and I need your help."

"I knew it!" shrieked Frankie "My earlobes have been itching like mad for the last ten minutes!"

Roxy began pulling Frankie along the tunnel with her. "Right, so I'm going to pretend to give Queen Bellissima the Seventh Stone, and I need you to—"

"Queen Bellissima? *Seventh Stone?*" Frankie gazed at her. "What kind of mess have you girls got yourselves into?"

"OK, the Queen Bellissima stuff – not our fault. And the Stone ... well, I've kind of had it in my pocket since yesterday morning, but in fairness, I thought it was just a free gift from a cereal box. Though I've got no idea how it got *into* the cereal box in the first place. Look, Frankie," Roxy went on as they neared the end of the tunnel, "we've got to pretend to give Queen Bellissima the Stone so she'll unhypnotize Jones."

"She's been hypnotized?"

"I don't know exactly. Whatever it is, the evil mirror tried it on me, too, but it didn't work." A thought quite suddenly popped into Roxy's head. "Oh! You don't think that's because I had the Stone in my pocket, do you? That maybe it protected me from the Dark Magic or something?"

"Oh no, dear, I don't think so," said Frankie. "The Witching Stones are completely inert until a spell

225

is performed through them. If you really want my opinion," he went on, patting her hand, "I'll bet any immunity you have is simply down to *you*, and that one-in-a-million mind of yours. You're a heck of a lot stronger than you think, dearie. And you *can* do this."

"I can. I can." Roxy was actually starting to believe it herself now. This was not the time for self-doubt. They'd reached the end of the tunnel and Bijou's room was – hopefully – the other side of this wall. Roxy opened her hand to reveal the pale grey triangular stone she was holding, and was rewarded by an awed gasp from Frankie. "So, if the Stone will magnify whatever spell you perform, maybe you could cast a massive spell on the evil mirror to trap Queen Bellissima inside once and for all?"

"Oh, my dear." Frankie looked downcast. "I love your faith in me, but you've seen my spells in action. It's no good being super-powerful if it's wildly inaccurate. Though, I suppose I can at least block any spell she hurls at us…" He thought for a moment and swallowed hard. "I'll try *Exodus Magicam, Exodus Magicam* – that's the most reliable spell-blocker I know. Stay behind me, dear. I'll do my best."

Roxy nodded, handed Frankie the Stone and then scrambled up through the hole in the tunnel wall.

## 25

"A-ha!" hissed the Dark Glass as soon as it saw Roxy appear. "The time was ticking! I'm so glad that you've returned. I think your friend was starting to feel positively spurned."

Roxy, dashing to Jones's side, was pretty sure her friend wasn't *feeling* anything at all. Her mouth was slack, her skin pallid and her eyes blank holes where two sparkling gems used to be.

"Jones," she said urgently. "It's OK. It's me. I'm going to get you out of this. We're a team, remember?"

"How sweet!" the Dark Glass chuckled. "And now I see you've brought *another* little chum…"

"Too right she has!" yelled Frankie, as he followed Roxy out of the fireplace. He planted his feet squarely on the floor, raised the Stone high in the air and pointed directly at the Dark Glass with his other hand. *"Magnificatus Diabolicum!"*

A luminous lilac light shot out of the end of Frankie's fingers at tremendous speed towards the Dark Glass.

There was an ear-splitting crash as the Glass shattered into a thousand – no, a hundred thousand – crystalline shards.

Roxy dived to the floor to avoid the explosion of glass, dragging a rigid Jones down with her.

"Didn't you say you were just going to *block* her magic?" she gasped to Frankie.

"I did, but then I got all carried away with the moment and tried something more complicated, an anti-Dark Magic charm ... but oh dear, oh dear," Frankie wailed. "I said **Magnificatus** instead of **Minimicatus**, didn't I? That was totally the wrong way round! Huge mistake! Huge!"

Something was emerging from the cloud of glass-dust that had been sent up by the shattering mirror.

And the something was *big.*

It was bright, too: giving off such a violent green glow that Roxy shielded her eyes. From behind her hand she could see a human face, still in the process of forming itself.

"Well, well," hissed a mouth from the middle of the face, as feline eyes and a long nose and striking cheekbones all began to arrange themselves in their correct positions. "You little fairy fool. Whatever have you done? Don't get me wrong: it's good for *me*. I'm here. I'm back. *I've won.*"

"Don't speak too soon, dearie." Frankie, his own face green with Queen Bellissima's reflected glow, raised his hand for a second spell, determined to fix his mistake. Light began to fizz at the end of his fingertips, forming a huge lilac ball. Even Frankie looked taken aback for a moment at how much more powerful his magic was now he had the Stone. "You're not protected by that mirror any more, Your Former Highness! So ... *Minimicatus Diabolicum!*"

The huge lilac ball flew through the air towards Bellissima. The moment it touched her glow, it bounced straight off, struck Frankie full in the face, and knocked him right back through the fireplace.

There was a brief, terrible silence.

"A sneak attack?" hissed Queen Bellissima. Her body shape was forming now, draped in the shimmering fabric of a purple gown. "You want me dead? How rude – I feel rejected. Of course, it failed. And now you're just one human, unprotected."

Roxy's brain ran through her options. Even if Bellissima's magic skills were a tiny bit on the rusty side after twenty years diminished to a mere cloud of

gas and locked up in a top-secret prison, she was still
– there was no way of getting around this – *a massively
evil super-witch.* Frankie's mistaken *Magnificatus* spell
had just made her even more powerful, and clearly
now a **Minimicatus** spell was useless against her.

But Roxy, of course, had something this massively
evil super-witch didn't have.

"Not unprotected," she said, darting to the spot
where Frankie had just been and grabbing the Stone
from the floor. "I've got the Seventh Stone, remember?"

This appeared to be the funniest thing Queen
Bellissima had heard in two decades. More alarmingly, as she shrieked with laughter, Jones began to
emit a flat, robotic *hahaha* of her own.

"Oh yes, you have the Stone," Bellissima cackled.
"But still, your situation's sticky. To *have* the Stone is
simple; it's the *using* it that's tricky. For let's be clear:
you're nobody. You get it? Catch my drift? You're
nothing but a silly child: no talent, skill or gift."

Which was when Roxy closed her eyes.

Because she did have a gift. She did have a talent.
And she knew what she needed to do. She needed to
conjure up something she'd once read.

It was going to be tricky, as she'd only seen it for
a mere second. And upside down. And it had mostly
been in Latin.

She needed the magic spell she'd read on Mortadella's phone screen, back at the Witch's Retreat.

The only other spell words she had ever heard had been Frankie's, and she already knew that *Minimicatus Diabolicum*, even when channelled through the Stone, was now too weak to work on the newly invigorated Bellissima. But Mortadella, surely, was the sort of serious-minded Magical Being whose spells would be *strong*, and *accurate*, and *effective*.

Roxy breathed in deeply and tried to visualize what she'd seen on Mortadella's phone.

Perhaps it was because she was panicking, but she couldn't see anything. Nothing at all.

She half opened her eyes and saw that Bellissima was moving towards her. Her beautiful lips were curled upwards in an unpleasant smile, and her black eyes glowed with the anticipation of doing something properly horrible.

"Hand it over," she murmured. "Do it now, and you'll still walk away. *You do not want to mess with me, I promise you. OK?*"

Roxy closed her eyes again.

*An easy upgrade for the highly skilled witch…*

This was it! Even if she wasn't skilled. At all. Let alone highly. Or a witch.

*Incantate hexabore…* This sounded promising, but

there was a third word and a fourth … what *were* they…? Roxy screwed up her eyes so tight that she could see spots dancing in front of the words she was trying to make out.

"*Do not dare to close your eyes!*" screamed Queen Bellissima. "How do you have the gall? Look upon my face, for I'm the fairest of them all!"

… **comestibi** … Right, now that last word was all Roxy needed. Her hand clutched the Stone, she was pointing the sharp end of the triangle straight at Bellissima…

Then, just as the witch raised her own hands to attack, Roxy remembered it.

"**Incantate hexabore comestibi penultarum!**" she yelled.

For a split second – a split second that felt to Roxy like a lifetime – nothing happened.

Then a sudden shaft of bright white light shot out of the Stone, heading for a startled-looking Bellissima. And Roxy knew, just *knew*, that the spell was going to work. But she didn't have time to enjoy this feeling, because the light had caused the Stone some serious kickback. A powerful shock zipped through her hand and all the way up her arm. It was so strong that it flung Roxy backwards, against the wall, where she knocked her head. She just had time to see the light hit Queen Bellissima smack in the chest before the sharp blow to her head sent her into oblivion.

And blackness.

## 26

**TWO DAYS LATER.**

"So let's run through it all again, Roxy. You were in Mrs Kettleman's doughnut shop – ignoring my direct order not to leave the Ministry grounds, by the way…"

"Again, Gretel, I'm sorry about that."

"… and while you were there, you saw Bijou Splendid have her head turned into a mango…"

"A pineapple, actually."

"… and because of that, you met your first-ever … ah … magical person…"

"My first-ever BOBI. Can you *please* just get your head around the fact I know about this stuff now?"

"… an *unlicensed* magical person called Francesca the Flotsam Fairy…"

"Yes. Look, G – I know you're a big deal at the Ministry, so if you could maybe have a word with someone about the whole *unlicensed* thing? Frankie's a bit disorganized, but he never intended to break the law."

"... after which you took it upon yourself, *this* morning, to take this Frankie to Bijou's bedroom so he could apologize..."

This part, obviously, was a bit of a fib, but Roxy was relieved she seemed to have got away with it.

"... whereupon," Gretel continued, "you encountered the spirit of evil Queen Bellissima in Bijou's dressing-table mirror, used the Witching Stone you happened to have in your pocket to perform a powerful spell to defend yourself, and in the process turned the evil Queen into a giant goji-berry-and-bran muffin."

Gretel spoke the last sentence very quickly and matter-of-factly, which made it obvious to Roxy that she was determined to gloss over the fact that all this had been achieved with the help of a Witching Stone. Roxy stowed this away for now, ready to use it when her sister was a little more off guard.

"Why *was* it a giant goji-berry-and-bran muffin?" Roxy asked now. "What I turned Bellissima into, I mean. Why not ... I don't know ... a buttered crumpet? Or a barbecue chicken wing? Or a pot of apricot yogurt?"

"Must have been the last thing you ate," said Gretel

235

briskly. "I only have a rudimentary knowledge of spells, I should point out, but there are some very basic ones that reproduce your last meal. From the days when food was scarce, I imagine, and you might have wanted to turn your empty lunch plate into a full supper plate, or feed a family of ten on one person's mashed parsnip." She got to her feet and marched smartly to the window to straighten the blinds. "Well, I suppose I have to believe your story, Roxy, though I still don't know *what* possessed you to bring an unlicensed fairy right into the heart of the Ministry!"

The fact that Gretel was talking, quite openly, about unlicensed fairies; the fact she hadn't changed back into her undercover loo-cleaner garb but was instead still sleek and glossy in her high heels and her red coat … Roxy's sister clearly wasn't bothering to pretend any more. The game had been up, in fact, since the first crazy moments after the explosion, when Roxy had been a little bit alert (among a whole lot of totally-out-of-it). Gretel – impressively only a few minutes late on Bellissima's trail – had been the first one into Bijou's room, barking orders at dozens of **SMOGs** behind her and using some amazing-looking zappy thing on the giant goji-berry-and-bran muffin – aka Queen Bellissima – to get it under a laser web. And Gretel had been the one who'd run to Roxy's side, taken her hand and said, firmly, into her ear, "You're all right now, Rox. I've got it all under control. You're safe. You're safe with me."

The loo-cleaner alias was over.

The question was: exactly how open and honest was Gretel prepared to be?

Alongside this, to be fair, was the question of how open and honest was Roxy prepared to be herself. She was fudging her story, however bad she felt about the half-truths and the careful omissions, because Gretel, quite evidently, did not know about Jones. Roxy had come up with the fib when she'd woken up in the hospital room only a couple of hours ago. It seemed the best explanation for it all: what she'd been doing in Bijou's room; how she knew so much about magic… And all while protecting Jones.

Jones, Roxy was as certain as she could possibly be, had somehow managed to slip away in the mayhem that had followed the explosion. As far as Gretel was concerned, therefore, *Jones did not exist*.

"Anyhow, we'll talk more when you're all better. For now, I should let you rest." Gretel came back to the bed to plump Roxy's pillow. "Now, a little later today, a lady called Mrs Smith is coming to visit you. Don't be alarmed, but she's going to have to do something called a False Memory Enchantment on you. It won't

237

hurt in the slightest, I promise, but all this stuff you learned from Francesca the Flotsam Fairy is rather dangerous for you to know. All right?"

"Well, no, not really, but I suppose I don't have any ch—"

"I'll come back later for that, but right now I have a pile of work to be getting on with. You've no idea how much chaos your escapade has caused us all! I suppose I should be glad that Minister Splendid hasn't fired me just for being related to you."

"Or because you stole the Seventh Stone from the Dodgy Old Clock," Roxy said.

Gretel froze. "What did you just say?"

This was the moment – perhaps the only moment, if Mrs Smith was coming to do that False Memory Enchantment later – for Roxy to try extracting the full truth from her sister.

"Look. You know I used the Stone to do that spell. And you haven't asked me how I got hold of it. Because – let's not pretend any more, Gretel – you already know *exactly* how. It was in the Proon Puffs packet. And the only way the Stone could have got into our Proon Puffs packet, in the first place, was if *you* stole it." Roxy didn't know if Gretel's attempt to gloss over her possession of the Stone had jolted her brain into this realization, or if she'd kind of known

238

it all along. "*You* had access to the Stone in Minister Splendid's office. The Proon Puffs were *yours*. It's not exactly rocket science, G!"

Gretel didn't reply. It looked as if she might have forgotten how to breathe.

"The thing I *can't* work out," said Roxy, "is *why*. I mean, I know you didn't take it for bad reasons – Diabolical reasons, that is. But it was such a massive risk for you to take it at all that I honestly can't think of *any* reason that makes sense."

Gretel sat back down on the chair next to Roxy's bed. She hid her face behind shaking hands.

"*I didn't know what else to do,*" she whispered from behind her closed fingers. "*I didn't know how else to keep you safe.*"

"Me? Safe? From who?"

"When I first heard there'd been a breakout…" Gretel put her hands down on her lap. They were still shaking. "I'm only afraid of one person, Roxy. I've only ever been afraid of one person, my entire life. And when Minister Splendid called me to his office to tell me, the other night, that there'd been a prison break, my first thought was: *she'll come to get us.*"

"Queen Bellissima?"

Gretel shook her head. "Worse. Far worse. You see,

Roxy, this … thing happened, to me and Han, when we were kids…"

"You were Hansel and Gretel. From the fairytale. Sorry, from the 'fairytale'." Roxy put the fingers of both hands in the air and made quotation marks. "You don't have to tell me, G. I know."

"YOU KNOW?" Gretel's eyebrows were higher up her forehead than any eyebrows had the right to be. "Did Frankie the Fairy tell you that, too?"

"No. I worked it out." This was *sort of* true. "Your names. Your freaky sugar phobia. Han writing entire albums about being locked in a cage by a witch… I mean, it's sort of impossible *not* to work it out, Gretel, once you know fairytales really happened."

"Wow." Gretel looked – for the first time in her life – a tiny bit in awe of her little sister. "You *really* need that False Memory Enchantment, and super-fast. I don't want you knowing all this stuff for the rest of your life. It's way too much to live with."

"So you wanted to keep me safe from the witch that kidnapped you and Han when you were kids?"

Gretel nodded. "The Gingerbread Witch," she whispered.

"And she escaped from the mountain prison too?"

Gretel shook her head. "She was never captured in the first place. They never found her when they were

240

rounding up the Diabolicals." Her words came fast, as if it was a relief to tell all this to someone who in a few hours' time wouldn't remember it any more. "We think she's deep, deep inside the Border Woods where her cottage once stood, but those woods are still way too dangerous to enter and go after her. They're the only part of the kingdom the Great Clean-Up couldn't touch. Oh, that was the programme Minister Splendid implemented, by the way, to clear Dark Magic out of the kingdom. *Don't* tell me Frankie the oh-so-convenient fairy told you about the Great Clean-Up, too," she added, exasperated, as Roxy failed to look surprised enough.

"A bit," admitted Roxy, "yeah."

"Terrific." Gretel rolled her eyes before continuing. "Well, the prison break multiplied the danger from Dark Magic a hundredfold. Trust me, I know too much about how these Diabolicals work to have the slightest doubt. Queen Bellissima intended to get her body and her powers back and then start spreading her Dark Magic tentacles over the country faster than you can say *Mirror, Mirror.* It would have given new strength to the evil in the Border Woods. Brought every Diabolical crawling back out from whatever rocks they've been hiding under for the last twenty years. The Gingerbread Witch among them. Now,

I never panic, Roxy. Everyone who knows me knows that I. Never. Panic. But this time…"

"You panicked."

"I panicked. When the office emptied out, I opened up the clock and took the Seventh Stone. Then, the night you came back from the Decontamination Zone, I used it to cast a protective charm over you. I've hardly picked up any magic in my job, as it happens, but I've always made darn sure I have one particular charm handy: a simple but powerful spell that wards off child-eating witches. I put the Stone into the Proon Puffs box for the night, because I knew it was a place nobody would ever think to look for it. That's the same reason, by the way, that I made sure the Dodgy Old Clock was put in Minister Splendid's office the very first day I took my job with him. Always remember, Roxy," Gretel said earnestly, "that the safest place to hide something is in plain sight. All the better, of course, if it's *in plain sight* in an office surrounded by armed guards, in a building *filled* with armed guards. But the Proon Puffs box felt as safe a temporary hiding place as any. Anyway, when I woke up I had to hurry to an emergency meeting, and I didn't have time to take the Stone back to the clock, and when I came back and it was gone…"

"You were worried you'd put it at more risk from Bellissima."

"I was worried Bellissima already *had* it! I can't believe how stupid I was to take it away from its secure hiding place! I was desperate, I suppose. The things the evil queen could do with that Stone, Rox. The things *any* Diabolical could do…" Gretel shuddered. "It's why only the tiniest circle of people know the Seventh Stone's location. A circle of people who can all trust each other." Her brow furrowed fleetingly. "One hundred per cent."

"But Minister Splendid isn't in that circle?" Roxy asked.

"Oh, Splendid's not a bad old stick, really. He'd never do anything truly harmful with the Stone. But he is…" Gretel pondered for a moment, and then sighed. "OK, I'm only telling you all this, Roxy, because you'll have it all put out of your head later today. The Minister is a teeny bit of a pompous twerp at times. I – *we*, in our tiny circle – worry that he might go around boasting about the Seventh Stone to the wrong person, a person who *does* intend harm. So no, he absolutely doesn't know the Dodgy Old Clock in his office is the Stone's hiding place. That it's *been* the Stone's hiding place for many, many years. He just thinks, thanks to me, that the clock is an ugly old antique that he has to keep on display because it was given to the Ministry by Queen Ariadne. And thank goodness, I've put the Stone safely back in there now. Just in time, too, because our group was already arranging to use it to cast a seriously powerful protective enchantment over the Kingdom, until Bellissima was caught. They wouldn't have been at all happy with me if I ended up having to admit I'd lost it."

This group – circle, Gretel had already called it – sounded the sort of thing that would have made Jones's head explode with excitement, Roxy thought, if she were here. She herself was bursting to know more.

"If there are still evil elements lurking in those woods," she asked, "why doesn't someone in your – uh – *circle* just use the Stone anyway? To cast that protective spell, or to seek the missing Diabolicals out?"

"Because it would have to be a real emergency to take that step," Gretel replied sharply. "These aren't insignificant spells we're talking about, Roxy. They're big spells. Huge, ancient spells. And the magic of the Seventh Stone isn't very stable. Spells cast with it can easily take on a life of their own. It's a colossal risk. None of us – *almost* none of us – want to do that unless there's no other choice."

There she was with the furrowed brow again, Roxy couldn't help but notice.

"So you've put the Stone safely back into the Clock now?" she asked.

"Yep. All safe." Gretel smiled with relief as she straightened Roxy's sheets. "You know, I can't believe I'm saying this, but I wish they didn't have to put the False Memory Enchantment back over you, Rox. It's kind of nice talking about some of this stuff."

"Will the Enchantment make me forget *everything*?" Roxy asked, watching her sister's face closely.

Gretel nodded.

"Pity." Roxy grinned up at her. "I wish there was the tiniest glitch in it so I could still remember my sister's secretly this totally awesome super-spy."

Now Gretel's smile broadened.

"You're pretty awesome yourself," she said.

Then her phone pinged.

"It's from Han," she said, glancing down at her phone with the particular smile she always used whenever her brother contacted her. "For you."

She swivelled the phone round to show it to Roxy. Just a brief text message: **Heard you turned a witch into a giant vegan muffin,** Roxy read. **Awesome work. Will deffo put that in my next song. H x**

Roxy had only just finished reading it when there was a second ping, and an ALL-CAPITALS, angry-looking message from Minister Splendid popped up on the screen.

**WHERE ARE YOU???? EMERGENCY MEETING (MY**

"I have to go." Gretel bent down to dust the top of Roxy's head with her lips before stalking towards the hospital-room door. In her heels and the scarlet coat, she looked magnificent. She stopped halfway out of the door. "I'll miss this," she said. "It's better than all the secrets."

"Way better," said Roxy, "than all the secrets."

And then Gretel was gone, closing the door behind her.

Which gave Roxy the opportunity, for the first time since she'd woken up, to slump back on her pillow and worry a bit.

About Jones, first and foremost.

All Roxy really knew was that Jones had got away.

The rest was there for her to imagine, and fret over. Had Jones come back to herself moments after Queen Bellissima's power had been broken, then slipped out of the Ministry as fast as she could? Was she now safely back in her attic above the doughnut shop?

Would Roxy ever see her again?

And there was another worry, too, smaller than the one about Jones, and not yet completely clear in Roxy's aching head. The outline of this worry was fuzzy, and blurred, but in a way this made it more concerning still. It felt as if it was lurking in the shadows.

Was it a worry about the at-large Gingerbread Witch, her brother and sister's deadliest enemy? Or was it something – or someone – else?

There was a light tap at the door; lunch must be on its way.

"I'm not hungry!" Roxy called out politely, but the door opened anyway. "Thanks, but no thanks," she said, a tiny bit less politely, as the trolley began to bump its way through, shoved inelegantly by a hospital orderly. "I'm a bit tired, and I'd rather just be alone."

"Not *hungry*?" the orderly snorted from beneath the baseball cap that was covering almost her entire face. "Are you for real? You've been out of it for two whole days, without so much as a sausage, and now I'm *actually bringing you a sausage*. All right," the orderly went on, whipping the lid off the plate on the trolley with a flourish, "I've seen better sausages. It's a pretty sad-looking sausage, when all's said and done. But still, it's a sausage. So it's definitely not to be sneezed at."

"Jones!" Roxy cried out. "It's you!"

"Yes, it's me, and will you keep it down a bit?" Jones hissed, pulling off the baseball cap and hurrying over to Roxy's bed. Her hair, now a shade of mushy-pea-green that only someone as beautiful as Jones could pull off, brushed against Roxy's cheek as she leaned down to give her a fierce hug. "You've no idea how difficult it was for me breaking into this place, and if I get discovered…"

There was a pointed cough from beneath her badly fitting white uniform.

"Forgive me," came Mirror's voice, "but I must object! Your use of *I* and *me* is hurtful and inaccurate: it should be *us* and *we*!"

"You saved Mirror!" Roxy gasped.

"Yeah, and I'm regretting it already," grumbled Jones. "Forty-eight hours of non-stop whining, it's been."

"You'd *think* she'd have been grateful," came Mirror's voice, "for the help I kindly gave. We wouldn't even *be* here if I hadn't been so brave!"

"You kept lookout over my shoulder while I jemmied a window!" said Jones. "Reflecting what's behind me isn't *brave*! It's pretty much the only useful thing a mirror can do."

"You jemmied a window to get in here?" Roxy asked.

"Oh, relax! Anyway, less about me, what about you! How about your totally epic braveness back there with the Stone? I mean, turning a massively powerful witch into a vegan muffin?" Jones gave Roxy a high-five. "Seriously, QG, I did not know you had that in you. I'll never forget that sight, when I snapped out of

248

whatever grim fog Bellissima had put me into. Good thing I was too busy working out how to get away, or I might have had a cheeky nibble! Actually, forget that. Those muffins were already seriously gross. How bad would they be with added chunks of evil queen?"

"Jones, look, don't get me wrong, I'm so glad to see you, but this is a special Ministry hospital. I don't think they want just anybody wandering around."

"Jeez, Louise," said Jones. "Didn't I teach you *anything*? You're far too trusting! This isn't a *hospital*. You're in the Decontamination Zone again!"

"*What?*"

"And it's where you'll stay for *weeks*, too, while they make absolutely certain you're not infested with all the magic you've come into contact with … I'd also be a tiny bit worried, if I were you, that they'll wipe your memory clean so you don't remember anything that happened with Bellissima."

"Put me under a False Memory Enchantment, you mean? Oh, they're definitely planning on that. Mrs Smith's coming to do it later."

"OK, so here's what you do: you insist she lets you see a lawyer, and claim it's against your human rights…"

"It's OK, Jones. I'm not worried. Well, not about that."

"*Not worried?* You don't mind forgetting all the awesome stuff I've taught you?" Jones's eyes were saucers. "All the awesome stuff we've found out together? You're *OK* if it all just turns into a soupy, swirly *mush* in that amazing brain of yours? Wow." She shook her head, already turning towards the door. "Right, well, I just stopped by to say congrats, Question Girl, and that I hoped we might hook up for another treasure-hunting mission one day, but if you're just going to let them *zap* you…"

"I'm not going to let them zap me," said Roxy.

"Yeah, you *say* that, but you'll be totally powerless against any enchantment Mrs Smith puts on you. So you'll be back to believing all the old rot, a brainless…"

Jones stopped talking.

Roxy had just opened her fist to show her what she was holding there.

And what she was holding there was a teeny-tiny fragment – barely bigger than a large grain of sea salt – of grey stone.

"You've got a weeny bit of the Stone," breathed Jones.

"I have."

"Is it a tiny bit that blew off it or something, when everything exploded?"

"It is."

"And are you going to hang on to it for dear life," Jones continued with a widening grin, "so that even when they *think* they've zapped you with a False Memory Enchantment, they haven't succeeded?"

"That's the plan," said Roxy. "Frankie mentioned a magic-blocking spell that might be powerful enough, if I've got some of the Stone, to hold it off. *Exodus Magicam*," she murmured. "*Exodus Magicam*."

The fragment of Stone in her hand was suddenly warm … very warm. It glowed bright white, as if ready for action.

*"Awesome,"* whispered Jones.

Roxy couldn't help giving her a grin. "I know! And then, *if* it works, and they eventually let me out of here, I can come and give the fragment to you, Jones. I know it's not the entire Stone, but you have to admit it's pretty incredible to have ended up with even a tiny fragment of it. And it'll be yours." She held out her hands. "You can do whatever you like with it. Display it as the first ancient artefact you ever collected. Use it to put a nasty curse on your stepfamily. Honestly, whatever."

For the first time since Roxy had met her, Jones's face turned a vivid pink.

"Look, for your information," Jones said, "I've

had … a bit of a rethink over the past couple of days. About … stuff."

"*I'll* say," Mirror interrupted cheekily. "She's been so stressed, you see. I swear she even *cried*."

"HEY! I did *not* cry!"

"I've heard her mutter, *Cripes, what if my only friend had died?*"

"Mirror, I swear on my life…"

"Oh, come on, Mirror, that doesn't sound the slightest bit like Jones," laughed Roxy.

"*Thank* you!" said Jones.

"I mean, I don't think I've *ever* heard her use the word *cripes*."

Jones glared at her.

"So you do actually care about someone else?" Roxy smiled.

"Maybe I do!" snapped Jones. "I don't see what's so funny about that! And that's got absolutely nothing to do with changing my mind about the whole revenge thing. It's not because I've gone *soft* or anything, in case that's what either of you are thinking! It's mostly just, since we saved the planet, and all that—"

"The country."

"… I've realized I've got more important things to do than take petty revenge on my stepmum and step-sisters. And seeing as I've probably got to go back and live with them again, for now at least, I'd rather just concentrate on getting the heck out of there as soon as I can."

"Oh, Jones."

"It's all right." Jones's chin lifted. "Turns out it's quite hard for a twelve-year-old to live on their own. Y'know, money and stuff. The manager of Mrs Kettleman's wants me to start paying for that room. Which is kind of a problem, 'cos I'm massively broke. And I can't go and live with Frankie, which is what I was sort of hoping, because of all those rules about fraternizing. Oh, and Frankie and Skinny are fine, by the way, in case you were worried. Frankie's back at home – all bandaged up and complaining about his hair being singed, but fine. And Skinny's staying with him for a bit, while they wait to find out if these stupid treason charges are going ahead…"

"Gretel may be able to help them with that," said Roxy. "And speaking of Gretel, I have *so* much I need to tell you! Stuff I've only just found out. So maybe you could stay with us for a while! I could speak to her, say you're a new friend and—"

"Don't worry about it. I'll think of something. Besides, it's actually *better*, probably, to live with people who make you totally miserable, because it makes you more *determined* to break free and save the world with your best buddy all over again."

Roxy opened her mouth to reply, but found that she had something stuck in her throat.

"Anyway, I can't stick around," Jones went on. "Way too risky to be here in the DZ. And anything you need to tell me, you'll have to tell me in a more secure location. You've said far too much already, you know," she added, darkly and a tiny bit patronizingly, which was Jones all over.

"You're telling me!" came Mirror's voice. "I *said*, dear Jones, I didn't care to risk it. But once again your stubbornness completely takes the biscuit!"

Jones rolled her eyes. "Mirror, for the last time, if you're coming back home with me, you have *got to learn to keep your non-existent mouth shut!* Honestly, I don't know why I've agreed to this ridiculous set-up."

Roxy was glad, though, that Mirror was staying with Jones, so that at least she would have *someone*, even if that someone was … well, Mirror.

Jones's hand was already on the door handle, "Anyway, I just wanted to say bye. And, obvs, thanks for saving my life and everything."

"Right back at you," said Roxy.

"And I'll be in touch," Jones said. "To get the lowdown on whatever your sis has been telling you.

And if I need your help again. If you'd *like* to help, that is."

"I'd love to," said Roxy. Quite suddenly something occurred to her. "Wait a sec. I've just realized! I don't even know your first name! I mean, there are millions of Joneses. If I only know you as Jones, how will *I* get in touch with *you*?"

"You won't need to. I'll contact you."

"Fine, but even so … we've been on this massive adventure, Jones, I'd kind of like to know the real name of the person I went with!"

Jones's lips pressed together so hard they were almost white. "Stupid name anyway," she muttered. "Always hated it."

"But what *is* it?"

"Um … it's Cinderella," Jones muttered. Then she raised her hand in a kind of half-wave, half-salute. "See you around," she added, "partner."

Then she flashed Roxy a brief, wild, beautiful smile.

And then she was gone, shutting the door behind her.

Leaving behind a blue-and-white trainer that had just fallen off her foot.

# ACKNOWLEDGEMENTS

Huge thanks are due to my magnificent agent, Helen Boyle, who has unflaggingly helped me steer Roxy and Jones in the right direction, aubergine motorbike or no aubergine motorbike. Without her, this book would simply not exist; she is a shimmering star. Huge thanks also to the fabulous Emma Lidbury and all her team at Walker Books, for editorial super-powers, for getting the jokes and for absolutely everything else in between. Thanks to Paola Escobar for bringing Illustria so beautifully to life with her gorgeous illustrations. And so many millions of thanks, more than they know, to Josh and to Lara, for making an ordinary old world feel like it just might be a little bit secretly magical.